# Reviews

"Absolutely a diamond in the rough. As Rose Spader recounts memories from her childhood, she also remembers stories passed down through generations of native New Mexicans. A wonderful read, I can't say it any better than the tag line - a great story of love, loss and redemption! The reader has a chance to understand the culture of New Mexico through the eyes of a true native!"
**--Leila Armstrong**

"Rose's father was brilliant and charismatic, but when drunk was neglectful to his family and physically abusive to her mother. Her mother was a free spirit with a 'pull yourself-up-by-the-bootstraps' attitude, who pushed herself and family to raise above poverty and hardships. Rose Spader has carved an amazing tale with honesty and love that affirms your faith in the human spirit. It's funny, sad, quirky, and loving. I was incredibly touched by it."
**--D. Prato**

# OVERTURNED BUCKET

*March 24, 2018*

*Enjoy the journey*

*Rose Spader*

# OVERTURNED BUCKET

## LOVE, LOSS AND REDEMPTION

A Historical Memoir Based on a True Story

ROSE SPADER

© 2017, 2015  *Overturned Bucket* by Rose Spader
                 Revised and Updated
Publisher: *Overturned Bucket LLC*
All rights reserved.
ISBN: 0996900004
ISBN 13: 9780996900003
Library of Congress Control Number: 2015918017
Overturned Bucket LLC, Albuquerque, NM

FOR EDUCATIONAL OR BULK ORDERS, please see overturnedbucket.com.

# ACKNOWLEDGEMENTS

It has been twenty-two years since I began journaling my memories and the memories of my family. Finally, having pieced the puzzle together, a novel of an extraordinary life from beginning to end unfolded. I have many people to thank for their encouragement, support, and sharing of their memories. I want to thank Carolyn Rose, Jessica Speck, and Kari Bovee for their enthusiasm and feedback. I am exceedingly grateful to Debra Speck, my steadfast writing coach, Katharine Boggess for editing, and Michael Spader for his artistic talent. To Denise Nourse, Matthew

Spader, and Mark Spader, thank you for visiting my birthplace with me and turning over gravestones of my past—I mean that almost literally. I want to thank my brothers and sisters and my many relatives for their memories, clarifications, and contributions. My kindest appreciation to the Philmont Museums and the Chase Ranch Museum of Cimarron, New Mexico for the photos of the Springer Mansion and of the Rolls Royce. Memoirs of Mabel Dodge Luhan, and books by Max Evans and Frank Waters were great sources of inspiration to this book. I want to thank my husband Stewart Rose, though he is no longer with me, for making this book possible. Above all, my parents deserve my undying gratitude. Their love instilled in me the ability to love unconditionally, the confidence to embrace humanity, and the fortitude to face life's varied challenges.

# TAOS

For my mother,
who walks with me eternally.

# CONTENTS

# Rosabelle Sandoval Ancestry

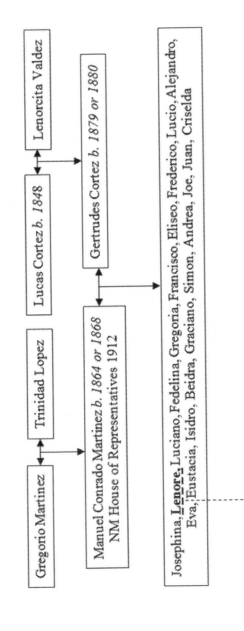

Gregorio Martinez — Trinidad Lopez — Lucas Cortez b. 1848 — Lenorcita Valdez

Manuel Conrado Martinez b. 1864 or 1868
NM House of Representatives 1912

Gertrudes Cortez b. 1879 or 1880

Josephina, **Lenore**, Luciano, Fedelina, Gregoria, Francisco, Eliseo, Frederico, Lucio, Alejandro, Eva, Eustacia, Isidro, Beidra, Graciano, Simon, Andrea, Joe, Juan, Criselda

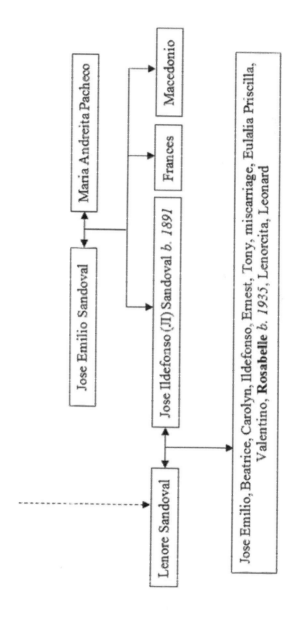

Jose Emilio Sandoval — Maria Andreita Pacheco

Jose Ildefonso (JI) Sandoval b. 1891

Frances

Macedonio

Lenore Sandoval

Jose Emilio, Beatrice, Carolyn, Ildefonso, Ernest, Tony, miscarriage, Eulalia Priscilla, Valentino, **Rosabelle** b. 1935, Lenorcita, Leonard

# FOREWORD

By Rudolfo Anaya

I t was a real pleasure to read Rose Spader's *Overturned Bucket*, a memoir whose riveting, realistic style held my attention from beginning to end. Spader's memoir is told by Rosabelle, the young Rose Spader. Rosabelle relates the stories of four generations of women from the 1880s to the present. Each woman plays a formative role in Rosabelle's life. The memoir also reveals many important nuggets of Nuevo Mexicano history of that culture-changing era.

Rose Spader was born eighty-one years ago in Taos, New Mexico, a village she fondly calls her Shangri-La. As such, she was witness to the tumultuous years at the turn of the 19th century, a time that changed New Mexico forever. This time of conflict began as Anglo-American homesteaders and entrepreneurs entered the northern New Mexico area after 1848. English became the dominant language, and men like Lucien Maxwell were able to buy and steal (mostly steal) indigenous land grants. The Maxwell land grant became the biggest in New Mexico.

Other famous, or infamous, personalities come to life in Spader's memoir. The Santa Fe Ring was organized around that time, and crafty politicians used the law to serve their purposes. A conflict of cultures exploded as the newcomers met the established Hispanos and Native Americans. Even the struggle for New Mexico statehood became part of the ensuing culture clash. In Washington D.C. an Anglo American congress would not grant statehood to New Mexico as long as the majority population was Spanish-speaking Hispanics. And Catholic to boot.

Many of these historical events form the background for Spader's memoir, but the real story centers around Rosabelle's relationship to her mother. It is the strength of the mother that helps Rosabelle survive the mean grandmother, the alcoholic father, and the displacement from home as the family has to move from place to place. Step by step, Rosabelle's journey tests her as the once stable society of her ancestry struggles to survive. Once helpful extended families begin to break down. Through all this it is the love and strength of Rosabelle's mother that is the guiding light. Her mother reminds me of the role my mother played in the lives of me and my siblings. I described her incredible strength of character and love in my 2016 novel, *The Sorrows of Young Alfonso.*

Rosabelle's family was patriarchal. The father ruled the roost, and as he gets caught up in the changing time that destroys his self-confidence, he takes to drinking. An entire generation of men lived through similar circumstances. Some readers may shy away from the reality Spader paints, but I see it as a valuable lesson in the evolution of women's liberation. Spader's story mirrors Rosabelle's struggle for equality. The story of the mother and Rosabelle's eventual knowledge of her liberation should be read by readers everywhere, especially in high school and university Women Studies classes.

In spite of the difficulties Rosabelle experiences, there is some joy in her life. She sees men build their homes from adobes, the cheapest materials the poor could afford. They work hard to provide sustenance for their families. The struggle to live and keep family together is at the root of this story. In spite of poverty and adversity, or maybe because of it, the Nuevo Mexicano culture survives and grows stronger. The values the ancestors taught assure Rosabelle that there is historical continuity and that the culture will evolve toward a better future. Spader's memoir is a testament to the culture that has retained its values in spite of adversity.

Rose Spader lived through a fascinating time. At eighty-one she shares her story with us. I found the same realistic and often poetic rendering of Hispano culture in Gloria Zamora's *Sweet Nuta*, a memoir that won the 2009 Premio Aztlan, a national literary award. The first printing of Overturned Bucket has already garnered one award, the 2016 State of New Mexico Heritage Preservation Award. How fortunate we are that these two gifted women have shared their stories with us. Two memoirs that should be read by every New Mexican. Students especially should read about this time of transition so they can compare it to their lives today. And I am sure these books will be read beyond our borders by those interested in our Nuevo Mexicano culture.

We need more memoirs like Rose's and Gloria's. The saying goes, if we do not write our history, others will write it for us. I wish these two talented storytellers all the best in getting their memoirs known far and wide. I am sure their books will be around a long time.

# PREFACE

Like the raging Rio Grande, this story cascades, meanders, and tumbles through time, whispering the voices of spirits long gone. On these pages are the bits and pieces garnered from my parents and relatives or as witnessed through my own eyes. In the beginning, I set out to understand more clearly what it was that gave my mother the fortitude to persevere against all odds. The story that unfolded in front of me brought to life a plethora of courageous people who bravely carved the beginnings of the Territorial Southwest. From the struggling homesteaders and advantageous entrepreneurs to the confluence of cultures that are in my family line, this story, true to the best of my memory and ability to convey, brings to life a bygone era.

I am grateful to the many authors whose work I studied to obtain detailed information and to my relatives who have shared their views. When stories differ from one account to another, the most plausible story has been used. When portions of a story are unknown, a likely interjection has been created and interlaced for the purpose of understanding. Also, though much of the dialog was in Northern New Mexico Spanish, here, for the ease of reading, it is written in English.

This story begins at a time when massive herds of buffalo thundered across the American plains, when the American Indian hunted and roamed freely—before the white man came to New Mexico. From the graves of infants to the peaks of true love, from the bonds of siblings to the devastation of alcoholism, with open arms, I invite you to visit my little village. Feel the damp marshes, smell the wild irises, and marvel at the beautiful summer sunsets. In the winter, walk on the white diamond-sprinkled blanket of snow as you gaze at the breathtaking Sangre de Cristo Mountains. Follow the banks of the Rio Grande out of abuse and prejudice and into a world of understanding and acceptance.

# PROLOGUE

## A BRIEF CULTURAL HISTORY OF NORTHERN NEW MEXICO

The fight for this territory began long before the United States staked claims west of the Mississippi. Ancient Indian tribes, unaware of the fate that awaited them, lived and thrived here—at peace with the land—never seeking to exploit it for individual gain. The native people molded and baked pottery of clay, made leather clothing from the hide of the American buffalo, and crafted baskets from peeled strips of the inner bark of nearby trees. They danced to the rhythm of the drum as they sang their ritual history.

Spanish conquistadors came to the Americas in the sixteenth century. The armored men on horseback conquered vast indigenous civilizations of the Americas with their primary mission to secure lands for Spain and save the "heathen" from hell's fire. It was in 1598 that Mexican-born conquistador descendant, Don Juan de Oñate, in search of gold and treasures he never found, led colonists across the Rio Grande into what centuries later would become the New Mexico Territory. There the conquistadors came upon Pueblo people living along the Rio Grande. Aggressively claiming the area, the conquistadors subdued and subjected the Indians to Spanish rule and Catholicism.

In 1680, all the Pueblo tribes that were established along the Rio Grande united in force, determined to drive out the Spaniards. Though victorious, the bloody revolt was not a permanent solution for the Pueblo Indian, and around 1696 the Spaniards returned, establishing several permanent settlements and missions throughout the area. Eventually a substantial Spanish population etched itself into the landscape near the Taos Pueblo and surrounding communities. The different cultures had no desire to assimilate. Adding to this early dissension, the Pueblo people and the Spaniards were in constant fear of Ute, Apache, Comanche, and other wandering nomad tribes raiding their supplies.

History tells us that after nearly three hundred years of Spanish rule, Mexico fought to reclaim its domain and won its independence from Spain. Meanwhile the United States, with the mindset of manifest destiny, had begun relocating the Indian people to reservations in the name of progress. Eager to expand its borders coast to coast, the United States initiated war with Mexico in 1846 in an effort to gain control of the Territorial West. After a series of small losses over the two-year battle, Mexico conceded more than half of its land to the United States. The signing of the Treaty of Guadalupe Hidalgo effectively ended the Mexican-American war in 1848 in favor of the United States. The Mexican border was then pushed south and west of the Rio Grande. Scattered Mexican settlers found themselves living outside their country's borders as the area quickly filled with English-speaking Americans moving into the newly acquired territory.

The Treaty of Guadalupe Hidalgo also provided for the protection of property and civil rights of Mexican citizens now living within the new boundaries of the United States. However, the American government made little or no effort to back up its promises. In order to keep their homesteads, these Mexican settlers, whether granted the land by the King of Spain or by the Mexican Government, were required to pay for their own surveys and legal procedures to perfect their titles in English—titles they already held. Few of these non-English speaking settlers could understand the language or afford the cost. Thus, it was easy for government officials, lawyers, railroad companies, foreign corporations, and investors to move in and take possession of tracts, large and small.

As the United States took control of the Territorial West, the Indian people in the newly acquired territory were relocated to isolated areas. Whether it was the government's desire to extinguish the main food source of the Indian people, or the incoming cattle industry's competition for rangeland, it would not be long before massive thundering herds of the American buffalo would be mercilessly massacred and left to rot.

By the end of the Civil War, railroad, mining, and timber industries were booming. Big companies and moneyed entrepreneurs moving into the area were not concerned with the established ways of the communities they occupied. Though these early entrepreneurs realized great gains through the exploitation of the people, the land, and the abundant resources, they were also the economic harbingers of modern New Mexico.

# PART I

*Chapter 1*

# SERENDIPITY

I look back to all the good things and the not-so-good things I've done. I have no regrets. It is my legacy to my family, to the world that continues regardless of my passing. I have seen the inside of poverty and of wealth, of devastation and of good fortune, but the most important lessons of life my mother taught me though she died just before my twenty-ninth birthday. From my humble beginning to my sitting here today, my life has been one of opportunity and freedom.

Nestled near the southern end of the Sangre de Cristo Range, with the snowcapped mountains to the east and the deep Rio Grande Gorge to the west, is the tranquil Shangri-La Village of Taos, New Mexico. For centuries, this charming and secluded village, like a settlement somewhere in Europe, has beckoned diverse cultures to its breast. It was here, in the year of 1935, in my grandmother's fastidiously kept home, that my mother, Lenore, at the age of thirty-nine, lay painfully birthing her tenth child. In the delirium of her labor, my life began.

My name is Rosabelle. Today I am eighty-one years old. I alone am left to tell this story. My parents and my brothers and sisters have all gone before me. I am a descendant of the Spanish conquistador Hernando Cortés, or that's what Grandmother always said. I have remnants of the blood and spirit of the Picuris and Tiwa Indian coursing through me. I have been told that even as a baby I exhibited an unusual desire for freedom and independence.

In my youth, Taos offered endless diversion. Happy, I ventured out into the fields close to our home. I can still remember the moist, earthy fragrance as I walked through the sprawling, spongy marshes with my feet sinking a little at every step. Tall growing grass hid me at play from my imaginary friends. Narrow trenches ran full of crystal-clear water cutting across domestic yards. With my hands in the shallow, cold water I could feel the thick moss and slimy pebbles.

In the middle of this small village, a few feet from the main road, was a pond where I spent my time chasing frogs or playing in the mud while my father fished, content and distracted.

"Gold and silver are hidden in those mountains, Rosabelle," my father told me. Time would tell me that many an ambitious man would turn his life upside down in search of such wealth.

Wearing snow long into summertime, the towering blue mountain ranges sealed the horizon. Wild purple irises danced in the breeze, and the songs of the magpie and playful blue jay created a magical ambiance for me. In the evening, I sat quietly watching the sun cast a yellow and orange incandescent glow across the white cotton clouds as they faded into the nights of my earliest memories. Through the screen door, I could hear my mother humming while she cooked our dinner. Other times, as my mother and I sat close together on the steps in front of our house, she would tell me scary cultural superstitions handed down for generations. Stories of the spells of the *brujas*, and the wailing sounds of *La Llorona's* ghost looking for her lost children, left me peering out of my covers in the night.

Much to my disappointment, we moved away from Taos when I was still very young. The work environment had been stalled by the Great Depression. My parents, struggling to provide for our family, were forced to move where they could find work. By the time I was eight our country had joined World War II and Albuquerque, with a military pilot training air base, had become a busy city. My parents quickly found work in the "Duke City," as they often called it in those days. It was a pivotal point for my family and for America.

The year was 1943. I remember sitting on the swing in our screened-in front porch in our new house. I was watching my mother and dad through the living room window, waiting for them to make a decision. My fingers crossed, I strained to hear their discussion as to whether or not they would allow me to, at eight years old, make the 130-mile bus trip to Taos alone. My parents had strict rules raising my older siblings, but by the time I was born they had lived through trying times, and they were tired and willing to give me free rein. Like a pony, I was allowed to frolic at will.

Having returned to Taos many times with my mother, I assured my parents I could make the trip by myself. Being a willful, independent child, I did not understand their objections. I thought my dad was willing but knew my mother was not. My mother speaking in Spanish, pleaded with my father, explaining her concern for my safety. Supporting my high-spirited personality, Dad took time to light his pipe. With long drawn-in breaths he pondered his response.

"*¿Por que no, Lenore?*" Dad said. "She misses her cousins. Why don't you just let Rosabelle go? It'll give her something to do this summer."

*Yes, why not?* I thought.

Mother wanted to argue further. She paused and looked in my direction. After getting up from her chair, she adjusted her apron. With a sigh she said, "She will have fun in Taos."

I jumped off the swing and ran into the living room leaving my doll and her blanket with my suitcase. I rushed to hug and kiss them both, not giving them a chance to tell me. Talking over one another's words, they cautioned me to stay clean and to be helpful to my aunts. Naive, kind, and gentle, my parents wanted to please me and wanted me to be pleasing to others.

Somewhat taken aback by my enthusiasm, my tall, shy father grinned and took my hand. He told me he would walk with me the nine blocks to the Greyhound bus station to buy the ticket. *"¿Qué? ¡Oh no, Papa!"* I quickly assured him with impassioned fervor that I could easily carry my belongings and buy my own ticket.

A glance from my mother released my dad from his decision-making obligation. Mother smiled in my direction. I kissed and hugged them both again, promising to be good.

Wearing my new homemade dress, my doll and her blanket under my arm and toting my suitcase, I was ready and in a hurry to leave—eager to see my relatives. As I looked over my shoulder to wave goodbye, the concerned look on my mother's face gave me a fleeting feeling of loneliness.

"Be safe, Rosabelle," Mother said, throwing me kisses.

At the depot, thinking like an eight-year-old, I reasoned that Taos was such a small town, the ticket person would not be aware it existed but he would know of Santa Fe. Feeling very adult and in control, I bought a round-trip ticket to Santa Fe.

In Santa Fe, I had to change buses and got in line to board for Taos. Carrying my doll and her blanket, I handed my ticket to the driver. "You're on the wrong bus, Little Miss," he said, pointing to another bus. Undaunted, I followed his instructions and again got in line. This bus driver accepted my ticket. I started on the second leg of my journey, happily anticipating two weeks with my relatives.

Sitting comfortably looking out the bus window, my jaw dropped open as I saw that the road we had taken into Santa Fe was the same road we were now on, but going back—the wrong way! After gathering my doll and her blanket, I left my seat to let the driver know I wanted to go to Taos, not Albuquerque. Nodding, he wheeled the bus off the pavement and onto the dirt at the outskirts of Santa Fe, miles away from the edge of town. He and I exited the bus and headed straight to the baggage compartment. After I identified my suitcase, he removed it from the compartment and placed it on the ground near where I was standing. He closed and locked the hatch and walked to the bus door. Without a word, the driver entered the bus, pulled the lever-arm closing the door, shifted gears, and stepped on the gas, leaving me in a cloud of exhaust.

**Manuel Conrado Martinez
NM House of Representatives
1912**

**Gertrudes Cortez Martinez**

# Chapter 2

# MARRIED AT THIRTEEN

## NEW MEXICO TERRITORY 1800s

Long before I was born, New Mexico was still part of the untamed territorial wilderness where the grizzly bear and the American buffalo roamed freely in the northern mountains and high plains. My great-grandfather, conquistador descendant Lucas Cortez, was born near the village of Taos, on June 6, 1846 during the Mexican-American War. Mother told me that at the age of sixteen he volunteered during the Civil War. When he returned from the war he married the young and beautiful Lenorcita Valdez. Great-Grandfather was a farm laborer and later worked as a cattle herder on the vast acreages owned by his father. For a time, he worked as an independent teamster.

On a snowy, blustery morning in the winter of 1890, Great-Grandfather Cortez, hauling lumber from a little town just north of Taos to the coal mines in Trinidad, Colorado, encountered a younger teamster at the Ponil Livery Stable struggling to hitch his horses to a loaded wagon. One of the lead horses reared and squealed, pawing at the wind. Great-Grandfather pulled back the brake on his wagon and jumped down to help the young teamster.

"Bad weather again today," Great-Grandfather said, grabbing the impatient horse's bridle.

"It's been a hard winter, sir," the young man said, and continued adjusting the harness. With the reins securely attached to the bridle, he threw the straps over the backs of his team and tied them to the handbrake on the side of the wagon.

Great-Grandfather introduced himself, unaware that the engaging young man standing before him would soon be his son-in-law. "Lucas Cortez," he said, extending a weathered right hand toward the young man.

Taking the offered hand with a firm grip, the young man responded. "Much obliged, Señor Cortez. Manuel Conrado Martinez, though people call me M.C."

"M.C., is it? You from around here?"

"Catskill, mostly, but headed to Trinidad today." M.C. pulled his weight up onto the high wagon seat.

Great-Grandfather warned the young man, "Keep an eye out. I just came through Raton Pass. Snow from yesterday's storm stopped the train."

"Thank you, Señor. I have good horses," M.C. yelled. Turning his attention to his harnessed team, he snapped the leather reins. M.C. headed out on his difficult trek, the horses straining in unison.

According to my mother, both men also hauled lumber for the railroad companies, as tracks were laid to reach the west coast. In the years to come, a friendship would develop between my Great-Grandfather Lucas Cortez and his future son-in-law.

The changes taking place with the introduction of the railroads and the increasing population provided ample work for the teamsters. In 1893, at the age of twenty-five, M.C. asked Lucas Cortez for the hand of his beautiful thirteen-year-old daughter, Maria Gertrudes Cortez. Gertrudes was born in Glorieta, New Mexico nineteen years after the Civil War Battle at Glorieta Pass. The oldest of four children, she entered marriage ignorant of the demands that would be placed upon her. It was a difficult start for the newlyweds, because an economic downturn in that same year caused the worst depression up to that time in the United States. Partly to blame were the overbuilding of railroads and the inclination of banks to overextend credit.

Young and naive, life changed quickly for Gertrudes. It is said that Grandpa M.C. had to find his young wife where she was playing and insist she come in to cook his meals. Marriage and the duty of cooking, cleaning and sewing for her family quickly transformed this child into a responsible adult.

It was February 8, 1896, in the emerging territorial town of Catskill, New Mexico that sixteen-year-old Gertrudes gave birth to her second child. The baby gasped her first breath at the slap of the midwife's hand and was wrapped in a handmade blanket and placed in her mother's arms.

*"Aquí está su hija, Señorita Martinez."*

Exhausted, the pain of labor behind her, Gertrudes reached out to hold the newborn, snuggling the infant close to her heart. Lightly stroking her newborn's cheek, she pressed the wailing baby's mouth to her breast. "Everything is going to be perfect for you, my precious baby," she whispered.

The proud father, M.C. Martinez, brought their two-year-old daughter, Josephina, into the room and knelt down near the bed so the sisters could meet. "She is beautiful!" he said. "What will you name her?"

"Lenore, after my mother. Her name will be Lenore."

The *curandera-partera* continued assisting Gertrudes, while in the kitchen, neighbor women were cooking and preparing food for the guests. Spanish townspeople brought food and gifts, crowding the dirt-floor adobe home. A birth was an honor, a blessing from God.

That evening, when the house was quiet and Gertrudes had fallen asleep, the *curandera* handed a small cloth satchel of herbs to Gertrudes' friend with instructions for steeping a tea to promote milk. M.C. went out the back door and returned carrying a gunnysack with three squawking chickens to give to the *curandera* for payment, as she had requested.

**Catskill, New Mexico**
**Photo Courtesy Palace of the Governors Photo Archives (NMHM/DCA), negative #014258**

At the time, the logging and coal mining frontier town of Catskill, named by a gentleman who said the place reminded him of the Catskill Mountains in New York, was burgeoning. Men worked together helping one another build their homes. And all pitched in to build a Catholic church.

Four hotels, a dance pavilion, and a ball-park were built by the entrepreneurs who employed many loggers and sawmill operators. People came from small villages and isolated homesteads to party in this hardworking, fun-loving community. A streak of coal had been discovered while timber was being harvested, and both were being hauled out by train as if the supply would have no end.

Baby Lenore's father worked at one of the five sawmills that also burned tons of wood by-product, producing charcoal that was in high demand. But before Lenore turned seven, the prospering boomtown had come to a grinding halt. In 1902, the natural resources were depleted and the railroad pulled up tracks. As the town faded into oblivion, M.C. Martinez packed his family's belongings, hitched the team to the wagon and took his family out of the once-lively town of Catskill, New Mexico.

Gertrudes was by then pregnant with her fifth child. Holding the youngest child on her lap, the three older children sat on the wagon seat between their parents. The family moved to different towns wherever M.C. found work in timber and mining: Brilliant, Dawson, Ponil, Raton, Springer, Sugarite, Yankee, even Trinidad, Colorado for a time. They travelled along rough trails, stopping only to eat and sleep. Sometimes as M.C. moved to his next job, the family stayed behind until a pregnant Gertrudes had given birth. M.C. and Gertrudes Martinez, my grandfather and grandmother, eventually arrived in Taos with their many children, eager to settle down and start anew.

**Young Lenore**

*Chapter 3*

# MATRIARCHAL SYSTEM

Dust could be seen miles away as weary cowboys, eager to find a place to rest for the night, approached with their thirsty herds. Disregarding their mothers' concern, children flocked to the edge of Taos village to watch the sunburned men riding through clouds of dust, wearing worn leather chaps, wide-brimmed hats, and handkerchiefs tied around their necks. The cowboys' cutting horses focused, keeping the bawling cattle tightly clustered and headed in the right direction.

One of Mother's highlights as a child was when her mother, Grandmother Gertrudes, allowed the children to sit on the front porch of their family home and listen to the cowboys sing. From their temporary camp, situated on a field owned by Grandpa M.C. and adjacent to the family lot, the children could hear the strumming of a guitar and the lonesome cowboys singing their sad songs. Lamenting their loneliness, the tired men gathered around their campfire near the chuck wagon to rest and eat food prepared over an open fire.

When she was about twelve, Mother had a crush on one of these cowboys. But Grandpa M.C., astute and concerned for his daughter acted quickly to squash the relationship. Mother watched for him whenever the wranglers came into town, but she never saw the young man again. Years later, Mother wistfully said she had always wished she could have married her first love.

While Grandmother Gertrudes was laboring the birth of more children, Grandpa M.C. was away most of the time working to support his family. Grandmother coped by asserting strong control over her large household. Determined to maintain an impeccably clean and organized home, she delegated responsibilities to her children. My mother, as the second oldest, became responsible for her siblings' care as soon as they were weaned. Whether it was changing or washing their diapers or tucking them in at night, Mother made sure their needs were taken care of. Her maternal instincts were well developed before she had children of her own, so her younger siblings often turned to her in times of need rather than risk punishment from their mother.

My mother's young life was limited to the dictates of her mother. The older children were responsible for keeping up with the maintenance of the house. Routinely, fresh calcimine was applied to the inside walls. All heavy bedding remained fresh with frequent visits to the local hot springs. And every Saturday, my mother and her sisters got on their hands and knees and scrubbed the rough wood floors using lye soap.

Even the outhouse was cleaned regularly, washing the seats and walls to free the place of spiders and to ensure proper sanitation.

The outdated Sears catalog, used in outhouses before the time of toilet paper, was kept in pristine condition. My sisters remember Grandmother's outhouse as the only outhouse without a foul odor.

"I hate doing this," Josephina said as they were killing spiders and wiping down their webs.

"Hurry up and wash the seats. You're going too slow," Grandmother yelled.

As an attractive, socially active woman married to a popular and successful business and political man, Grandmother Gertrudes was well liked and respected by her peers. She spent much of her time at the church helping the priests— organizing charities, soliciting volunteers, dressing the altar, or merely visiting with the clergy. A special room in my grandparents' home was kept in immaculate condition. Reserved for club meetings and guests, the children were forbidden from entering this room other than to clean. But no matter what extra effort was needed, all chores had to be completed before Sunday, the day of rest, according to Grandmother's religious beliefs.

When the children did not meet her expectations, Grandmother was stern and quick to punish—sometimes she took things too far.

From the open kitchen door, Grandmother Gertrudes watched her five-year-old struggle in the cold. "Fedelina," she yelled angrily, "it's going to be dark before you get all the buckets filled!"

Fedelina stood on her toes and stretched to reach the rope hanging from a wheel-pulley above the well. Hearing her mother's voice, she picked up two filled buckets and hurried into the kitchen. With each step, water splashed onto the floor. As Fedelina placed the buckets on a bench along the kitchen wall near the black wood stove, she turned to go back to the well for more.

Enraged by the spilled water, Grandmother grabbed her little girl and thrust her head into a bucket of water, holding her submerged while Fedelina squirmed frantically. Fortunately, both my mother and Josephina, her older sister, bravely intervened and pried the bucket away from their mother to save their little sister.

Mother tells me she and her sisters always looked out for each other, but it was rare that they stood up to their mother, fearing the possibility of further aggravating her. Even neighbors who may have witnessed use of harsh discipline by Grandmother did not interfere.

Grandmother had to take on adult responsibilities at a very young age and she had no awareness of work that was too difficult for a child. She enforced a strict code of silence in the family and she was contemptuous of her children voicing any feelings that expressed a need or implied a weakness.

As adults, my loving, kind-hearted aunts did not talk about their mother. Whenever the topic came up, it was with reluctance that they would admit to any of the abuse they received at my grandmother's hand. Generally they hid behind a poor memory. Respect for their parents was unequivocally instilled in my aunts. And they felt it was not for them to question or make judgment concerning their parents' actions. Though Grandmother's actions may have doomed her daughters to be self-sacrificing, reticent adults, it also instilled in them an enriched depth of empathy.

The only person Grandmother did not override was her father. One day Great Grandfather, Lucas Cortez, rode his horse to visit his daughter. As he approached the house he witnessed Grandmother Gertrudes shoving her young son's head into a manure-filled barrel.

Eight-year-old Luciano had been cleaning the chicken coop, raking up the droppings and placing them in large wooden barrels to ferment and be used as fertilizer. His mother, unhappy with his slow progress, took him by the nape of the neck, and stuffed his face into the manure.

So engrossed in her effort to punish her son, Grandmother did not hear her father frantically pleading. *"Gertrudes, por Dios déjà lo ir."* For the love of God, he begged, let the boy go!

He dismounted from his horse, and threatened her with his crop in an effort to prevent his daughter from suffocating his grandson. Grandmother angrily dusted off her apron, turned, and stormed away.

Great Grandfather took a sputtering and crying Luciano to the well and helped him wash the manure from his face. "You're a tough young man," Great Grandfather said, patting his grandson on the back.

Just as Mother was expected to tend to the children, Josephina was required to take on the responsibilities of the kitchen. One evening as Mother helped her older sister clean up after dinner, Josephina dropped the lid to the sugar bowl. The girls looked at each other apprehensively as Josephina bent down to pick up the broken pieces.

Grandmother's face flushed red as she reached for the handle of a cat-o'-nine-tails hanging on a large nail near the kitchen door. Josefina cowered, raising her arm for protection as Grandmother cracked the whip. With time and ointments, the welts that covered Josefina's body healed, but the tip of one of the whip's tails had caught the corner of one eye, and her vision was altered for life. Grandmother never expressed guilt or regret for her unusually heartless and cruel behavior.

Grandmother did not talk to her children about dating or sex, the difference between boys and girls, or the changes that take place as children grow into adulthood. Even so, no child at the age of thirteen is totally ignorant of certain biological facts—that is, no child except my mother. As a young girl, when she found blood on her undergarments, Mother ran to the nearby creek to wash it away. In her ignorance, she feared the bleeding indicated some horrible sin she had committed. She worried that if it were not punishment for sin, it had to be a bad disease that would most likely result in her death. The cold, crystal-clear water did not help my poor, bewildered mother. As the bleeding continued, she agonized that telling her strict, formidable mother would certainly bring about harsh punishment.

Mired in this desperate predicament, she finally determined that her only alternative was to go to her mother. Mother timidly confessed her condition. When she did not receive the condemnation she had anticipated she was baffled. Instead, she found her mother ready and eager to enlighten her of the curse that befell all women.

Projecting disgust, Grandmother Gertrudes piously articulated the condition with a hint of accusation clouding her voice: "Stay clean and be quiet during this time. You don't want to draw attention to yourself."

Handing her clean, neatly folded white rags she gave instructions on the proper way to fold a rag, how to secure it with safety pins to an elastic band, and how to wear the band under her bloomers. Grandmother showed Mother how to wash the soiled rags, first in cold water, then in soapy hot water and then rinsed in vinegar-water, and finally, the proper way to hang the rags on the clothesline.

"Women are evil from birth," she told Mother, proclaiming God was angry because Eve tempted Adam with the apple. She did not mention Adam's lack of responsibility to keep God's commandment in spite of Eve's request. Grandmother likened the women's monthly curse to the black race, telling her daughter that their dark skin was a mark from God to display to the world they had disobeyed Him. Mother was repelled and confused by this abhorrent, erroneous information.

Grandmother also advised my mother to maintain an attitude of servitude toward men. Before women's liberation and the progress toward equality between the sexes, it is not difficult to visualize the steel-plated shawl of ubiquitous guilt effectively bestowed upon my mother. Despite these limiting expectations, Mother did not have a presumption of being better than or not as good as anyone else and she saw no class or race distinction. Mother respected the responsibility of women serving men, but did not believe men were superior. She believed in the essence of challenge and action to be solely an individual's responsibility.

Grandmother seemed to hold the woman's curse as an excuse to demean her daughters on a regular basis. On one particularly cold winter morning, Eustacia, one of my mother's younger sisters, found that through the night her monthly period had started. She was seventeen years old and worked in town as a seamstress in a dress shop. Fearing she would be late, she did not take time to wash her soiled garments before leaving for work. Instead, she tucked them neatly under her bed and planned to wash them at the end of the day.

That evening, as Eustacia was getting ready to leave work, a customer came into the shop needing her attention. This, of course, made Eustacia late getting home, and this presented a problem. Grandmother had no leniency for anyone being late for the evening meal. Every day the table was set with enough food to feed their large family, plus occasional visitors. Once food was consumed, the men were free for the evening to relax, smoke, and feed their egos or indulge their social life.

The women were not allowed to join. They put the little ones to bed, cleaned the kitchen, and replenished the wood and water needed for the following day. The routine was sacrosanct. From dawn to dusk the women were busy.

That evening, as Eustacia rushed into the house, the entire family was already sitting at the dinner table. She quickly hung her coat and took her place. Nervously, she awaited the reprimand for being late and was happily relieved when nothing was mentioned. Had she been admonished for being late, it would have been mild, by comparison, to what actually happened. The family assembly continued to share their day's activities and indulge in the evening meal—that is, everyone except my grandmother.

Grandmother got up from the table and returned holding my aunt's soiled clothes in front of her for all to see. In a loud, accusatory voice she assaulted her daughter, hurling the soiled garments across the table at her face. "You disgusting, vile girl!"

With the exception of my grandmother's rage, silence engulfed the room. Shame and embarrassment permeated every soul. All action was suspended in midair, and endless seconds passed before the family could recover and continue their meal.

Frozen in her chair, Eustacia bowed her head in shame. Everyone sat immobilized and quiet, knowing it was not wise to compromise Grandmother's stand. In those days, a woman's menstrual period was an unmentionable subject— even in private it provoked embarrassment.

Grandmother's disciplinary tactics reinforced the notion held at the time of a woman's inferior position. She made it difficult for her daughters to interact with their father and their brothers, and later, husbands and sons, with confidence and a sense of equality.

Likewise, their male counterparts developed a stronger sense of unfettered superiority as became apparent one day, just before a dance: Conrado, given his father's middle name, was waiting for his sister, Fedelina, to iron his shirt. Young Conrado loved to party. He was good looking, a "ladies man," and an excellent dance partner.

After placing the hot, heavy iron back on the stove top, Fedelina handed the shirt to her brother, "Your shirt is ready, Conrado."

Conrado held up the shirt to inspect it. He noticed wrinkles around the cuff and threw the shirt back at his sister. "What's the matter with you, *Pendeja*? This shirt looks like s—t!"

Grandmother, supporting her son's actions and sympathizing with him, reprimanded her daughter. With her hands on her hips and a menacing look on her face, Grandmother chastised Fedelina, "Iron it again and hurry! You're making him late."

It would not be long before Conrado would have more to worry about than the wrinkles in his shirt. He became a lineman for the public service company and had complained to management that his leather safety belt was frayed and that it needed to be replaced. While working near Ranchos de Taos, high on a utility pole with live wire, his belt suddenly broke. To save himself, he grabbed a wire and was electrocuted, falling to the rocky edge of the Rio Grande.

He was pronounced dead at the site. But by the time they got him to the hospital, he had a pulse.

After much medical attention and fortitude on his part, my brave uncle returned home crippled, never to dance again. Mother improvised some of his clothing with zippers, attaching loops to the tabs so that he could grasp the loops with his gnarled fingers.

It pains me to think of the difficult childhood my mother and her siblings lived. I am also saddened for my grandmother, considering the demands placed on her. I question in my heart how it was for her. Was her life out of control or was she just devoid of empathetic feelings? I do not know, but I choose to respect her strength. Death of women and infants during childbirth was frequent in the harsh territorial life. It was an unfathomable marvel that Grandmother Gertrudes was able to survive the pregnancies and birth of twenty children and raise fifteen of them to adulthood. Moreover, she kept her children well dressed, well fed and taught them self-discipline that would serve them well over their lifetimes.

The ignoble position imposed upon women of my mother's day, combined with the harsh, strict discipline Grandmother exercised, left a long path of hard-working, hard-drinking men and submissive women. My mother was never able to totally rid herself of the inheritance of a women's inferior position—an inheritance she passed on, without intention, and to a lesser degree, to her own children.

To my knowledge, while Grandmother's marriage was contentious, Grandpa M.C. was not abusive in dealing with his wife. We can only speculate that the trauma of a marriage at thirteen and the birth of twenty children could have caused a deafening of her compassion.

However strict, Grandmother Gertrudes was indulgent of her sons, and to some degree, the grandsons she raised when she was older. My cousin Epifanio told me that one day, his mother, Tia Fedelina, sent him to the clear water ditch near their home. She handed him their last bar of lye soap, told him to bathe and wash his hair, and to be careful with the soap.

After getting to the ditch Epi put the soap near the water, removed his shoes, and rolled up his pant legs. He hung his shirt on a tree branch, picked up the soap, and stepped into the icy cold water. Bending down to wet his hair, the soap slipped from his wet hands and floated down the ditch. After many futile attempts to retrieve the soap, he nervously returned home to face his mother.

Tia, losing her otherwise patient demeanor, reached to grab Epi, determined to spank him. Evading her grasp, he took off running toward Grandmother Gertrudes' house. Hearing Epi calling for her, half out of breath, Grandmother met him on the front porch with a protective hug.

"I lost the soap in the river and Mother is going to spank me," Epi cried into Grandmother's apron.

Fedelina, in hot pursuit, approached Grandmother's house. Grandmother angrily scolded her daughter and forbade her from punishing her grandson.

Obviously, Grandmother was not kind toward the women in her domain. When her daughters-in-law turned to her for advice, support, or sympathy when encountering hard times—or the wrath of an angry husband—Grandmother expressed disdain with comments such as, "I don't blame him. It's your fault he treats you badly." She ostracized her in-law daughters, voicing her resentment of them openly to her sons.

Life expectancy of people in the Territorial West at that time was short, but my Grandmother's brother, Cruz Cortez, married a younger woman and at the age of seventy, fathered my cousin Pancho. Though only sixteen years younger than I,

Pancho is from the generation before mine. Pancho has told me that he and an uncle visited Grandmother Gertrudes in Taos when Pancho was eleven years old. She invited them into the kitchen and chatting happily, asked about the relatives. She pulled fresh bread out of the oven and served them hot bread with fresh-churned butter and chokecherry jam. He remembers her as being very nice.

Some of my male cousins talked about how Grandmother Gertrudes, or "Mama Grande," as they affectionately referred to her, taught them how to chop wood, remove and straighten out nails from old lumber, and set out vegetables from the garden to dry on the rooftop. Grandmother was forthright, organized, and highly resourceful. And she was not afraid of hard work.

For the most part, my cousins speak kindly of my grandmother and are grateful to her.

Out of all the men in the family, Grandmother's strongest affinity was for her father. Great-Grandfather Lucas Cortez is reputed to have been a responsible and wise man who taught his children to be independent. Mother says he was a hardworking man who bravely faced frontier challenges. He was a storyteller, often regaling his family and friends with tales of his varied and, at times, dangerous adventures.

One day, Great-Grandfather and a group of men were hunting a troublesome grizzly bear. Hungry, after coming out of hibernation, the silvery bear was threatening ranchers and their families. It attacked cattle and sheep, drank from their water troughs, and ravaged through their farms.

But, Great Grandfather and the other ranchers knew the habits of the grizzly. They set out to track down the indomitable troublemaker by following his scat. I can only imagine the look on their faces when they heard some huffing, twig-snapping sounds and turned to see the huge grizzly lumbering down the hillside towards them. The charging bear stopped a few feet from the petrified men, stood up and, swaying side-to-side, opened his large jowls and let out a terrifying growl. In an instant he lunged onto Great-Grandfather's back, knocking him over and pinning him down with his large, clawed paws. The ferocious bear mauled my poor great-grandfather to death before the bullet wounds inflicted by his companions finally killed the beast.

The loss of her father brought Grandmother to her knees. According to my mother, Great-Grandfather was loved and respected by his family and is remembered as being a rugged, adventurous man. My cousin Pancho's son, Lucas Cortez, is named after my brave great-grandfather and carries on his name.

*Chapter 4*

# TRAPPING, MINING AND LOGGING

While Spain owned most of the Territorial West in the 1700s, France owned the Midwest from Canada to the Gulf of Mexico. Many French-Canadian people came to this area during that time and even after the United States had purchased the huge Louisiana territory from France. The Louisiana Purchase gave the United States access to continue its westward advancement.

# TRAPPING, MINING AND LOGGING

The Louisiana Territory, at that time, included northeastern New Mexico, just to the outskirts of Taos. By the time Mexico had reclaimed the New Mexico Territory from Spain during the Mexican War of Independence, Taos had become a major trade location, which was accessed by the Santa Fe Trail. Many trappers and mountain men, wearing raccoon pelt caps and carrying muzzleloaders, came to the area to hunt and sell their hides at the Taos Trade Fair. Meanwhile, other resources were discovered. Digging for gold and minerals, logging timber, and grazing large herds of sheep and cattle took over as the fur trade subsided.

One of the most memorable entrepreneurs to come out of this period was Lucien B. Maxwell, a French fur trapper from Illinois, who had come west to make his fortune. His life had a huge impact on Northern New Mexico and on those of us, in the generations since, who lived and still live in the area.

Maxwell, through marriage, inheritance, and ingenuity, owned the largest piece of property ever owned in the Americas by a single individual at that time—the 1.7 million acre Beaubien-Miranda Mexican Land Grant. The entire Mexican land grant, mostly unpopulated land, rich in untapped gold, copper, coal, and timber, unbelievably belonged to just one man and his wife. The breathtaking mountain views, streams teeming with fish, hillsides alive with game, and vast acreages of grazing land for animal husbandry and farming, filled Maxwell's aspirations beyond his wildest dreams.

Maxwell grew his enterprise by charging fees for the use of his land, including grazing, water rights, mining, timber, and trapping. He processed multiple lease claims for the exploration of precious metals and coal and he successfully fought a multitude of asserted claims initiated by past owners and scattered Mexican settlers who held valid titles to parts of the same land.

Maxwell's private ranch worked an estimated 40,000 sheep, 10,000 cattle, and 1,000 horses and mules. He became an important supplier of beef, mutton, and grain for the United States Army and for the Navajo and Mescalero Apache tribes, confined and deprived of their hunting grounds at that time.

Colfax, which then included most of the area of the Maxwell Land Grant, became a county in 1869, and Elizabethtown became the first county seat in the New Mexico Territory. Maxwell was elected probate judge. In Cimarron, he was appointed postmaster and Federal Indian Agent.

At one time Maxwell also owned a bank and a hotel. Through the years, he sold large portions of his land to adventurers looking to become ranchers. At the age of fifty-two, due to the challenges of managing the huge grant, Maxwell sold what was left of his grant to foreign corporations, retaining only the property surrounding his home and some mining ventures.

He eventually moved to Fort Sumner and died there in 1875, not yet fifty-seven years old. It was six years after his death that Billy the Kid was killed by Pat Garrett in Maxwell's Fort Sumner house, which his son had inherited. Billy was buried a few feet from the grave of Lucien B. Maxwell.

Meanwhile, the Northern New Mexico grant had become the Maxwell Land Grant and Railroad Company. Demand for ties and wood beams for the railroads and mining industry made it easy to obtain government tree-cutting permits to harvest lumber on the Maxwell Land Grant and surrounding mountainous regions of the territory.

It was an opportune time for Grandpa M.C. to open a lumber company. The Forest Service marked the trees to be cut, and men used either single axes or two-handled saws to fell the timber. The rough logs were de-limbed by hand, using wide-blade, short-handled axes and made ready to haul to the mill. It was a labor-intensive and dangerous occupation and injuries were frequent. Sometimes there were fatalities.

Temporary camps were built to house the loggers. At times Grandpa's family lived at the camp. When the time came to move the camp, the last few logs, one-by-one, were fastened to a horse and dragged down the mountainside to the mill. My cousin remembers, as a boy, he would ride on the log as the horse pulled it. At the sawmill, the log was released. The trained horse returned to the cutting site for another log. Large quantities of felled lumber were transported by horse-drawn wagons, which Grandpa, years later, replaced with lumber trucks.

Grandpa M.C.'s office was in a back room of the company store. From this office he managed his business—negotiating contracts, hiring, firing, and handling financial transactions. When supplies were needed to restock the shelves, Grandpa went to town and returned with inventory. Loggers bought food and necessities from the company store using credit against their paychecks.

I can imagine a tired lumberman named Joe coming into the store, looking around anxiously to find the clerk.

"What can I do for you, Joe?" the clerk would say, standing up from behind the counter.

Joe would shift his weight and scratch his head before responding. "Juan, do you think Mr. Martinez could extend my credit? I need to pick up some supplies."

Grandpa would come out of his office, "Joe, you're behind on your payments already. You know I'll have to charge you interest."

A nervous Joe would take time to rub his right hand on his pants leg before reaching over the wood-plank counter to shake hands with his employer. "Much obliged, Mr. Martinez. I'll be able to catch up next paycheck."

I don't know if my grandpa ever employed someone named Joe, but I have been told that Grandpa M.C.'s company store was quite profitable. But as big-business lumber companies came into the territory, permits for independent loggers became scarce. In 1905, the United States Government intervened to regulate and save the natural resources, making cutting permits even scarcer. Foreseeing the limitations to his business, Grandpa pursued a more active role in politics.

My grandpa, Manuel Conrado Martinez as he was known politically, was born in Ponil, on December 25, 1868, during the aftermath of the Civil War. Grandpa M.C.'s father, Gregorio Martinez, fought in the critical battle at Glorieta Pass. As confederate soldiers opened fire on the Federal Garrison at Fort Sumter, President Lincoln responded by calling out the militia.

Slaves were freed and the secession was squashed, but more Americans died fighting this bloody civil war than died during all the other American wars up to and including World War II.

Grandpa M.C. fought his way out of poverty, retaining the humility of a humble beginning. Before marrying my grandmother Gertrudes, he had developed a reputation as a reliable teamster. A self-educated man with progressive insight, he was keenly aware of the ongoing fight for land and cultural identity. He was not afraid of the future and was determined to make a difference. Grandpa M.C. became a highly-respected leader in Northern New Mexico.

Social friends of Grandpa, Doc Martin and Republican State Representative Frank Springer, brought him into the political circle, further encouraging his interest in politics. In 1910, Grandpa M.C. was appointed School Director for the

8th District of Colfax County. When New Mexico attained statehood in 1912, Grandpa M.C. was elected to serve as the Republican Representative from Colfax County. While a member of the House of Representatives, he served on five different committees: education, liquor, traffic, penitentiary, and public institutions, and highways.

Grandpa M.C.'s political career continued even when his elected term as a representative ended. He was appointed Deputy Sheriff for Taos County, making him thereby the executive officer of the court and the police officer of the town. Aided by his lieutenants, Grandpa executed orders given by the court. The wardens and prisons were under his charge, and he could remove his lieutenants or the wardens for legitimate cause. The justices, sheriffs, and county clerk jointly administered the law of the district, and the sheriff was allowed to enter the town hall bearing arms. Years later Grandpa was appointed Taos Marshal.

Grandpa M.C. was a serious man with a good sense of humor and ethical convictions, who did not smoke or drink. The scope of his friends and associates was large and included all segments of the population in Taos, Santa Fe, and surrounding communities. As a knowledgeable leader, he was called upon to mediate in litigations involving land rights and civil disputes and was frequently asked to read the tribute at funerals.

My mother told me that Grandpa M.C. was a wonderful square dance caller. Grandmother Gertrudes and the children would accompany Grandpa to the dances. The boys carried baskets of food, the girls dressed in their gathered skirts with ribbons in their hair, and they all vied for favorite positions on the plank seats of the horse-drawn buckboard. Grandpa, a colorful handkerchief tied around his neck, would stand on the wooden platform next to the fiddler, clapping his hands and stomping his foot as he called out the dances.

In contrast to his successful political and social life, Grandpa's marriage was at times acerbic. My maternal grandparents were independently successful people, but their union was quarrelsome. Both stubbornly held dear to their individual opinions. Grandpa's ambitious involvement in the community conflicted at times with Grandmother's strict, unyielding nature, which created discord in their marriage.

Unlike Grandfather, Grandmother did not accept the mixed cultures and the new governing laws of the United States. She refused to acknowledge the inevitable evolution sweeping across her village. Grandmother understood the

English language but never spoke it. She spoke to her English-speaking grand- and great-grandchildren only in Spanish. Grandmother was confident in her opinions, forceful in her actions, and emphatically unyielding to change. She saw no need for her daughters to learn to read. They would not need an education to bear children. Education was not needed for her sons either. Their work was with their hands. She was outraged if her children attempted to learn English, feeling it would diminish their Spanish heritage, which she considered pure.

Mother tells me that Grandpa spoke to his children in English when not in hearing range of his wife. Outside the house, where Grandmother could not hear, Grandpa encouraged my mother to address him with Anglo-American names in order to practice her English.

While collecting eggs from the coop, Mother would timidly address her father as he was saddling his horse. "Good Morning, Mr. Brown."

"Good Morning, Miss Martinez. How are you today?" He would respond, as he bowed toward her, tipping his hat.

"Very well, thank you, sir."

Every so often Grandpa would introduce new essential phrases and new mannerisms, enabling his children to feel comfortable conversing in English. A good and supportive father, he had high expectations for his children. Mother said when she was young she wanted to be a schoolteacher. My cousin Bertha tells me Grandpa had an uncanny ability to find his grandchildren on their way home from school, eager to hear what they had learned that day.

My mother gravitated to her father's belief in integration, receptive to his prediction that, ultimately, all people would become one race. Mother loved her heritage, and no one could have been more proud of her ancestors. But for her to progress, she knew it was necessary to accept—in fact to actively embrace—the new language and the new ways.

Disregarding Grandmother's harsh nature, I am proud of my strong, determined maternal grandparents. Grandpa M.C.'s intelligence, striking hazel eyes and impressive stance, alongside Grandmother Gertrudes' fashionable attire and disciplined, capable ways, made for a good-looking, successful public couple. But the children born to the union witnessed the many varied shades. Grandpa's involved and supportive ways could only partially alter Grandmother's severe, astringent behavior.

The favoritism Grandmother showed toward her sons and the indifference she expressed for her daughters created a strong, caring bond between my grandpa and his daughters. He understood their challenges and helped them through trying times.

I remember that on our visits, Grandpa would look at me with a big smile. Sometimes when I needed my busy mother's attention, Grandpa, referring to me as "Donkey Ears," would tousle my hair and tell me not to bother my mother. *"Orejas de burro,"* he would say. *"No se moleste a mi hija."* It was his way of acknowledging the stress placed on my mother by the strict environment.

I find my grandmother's notion that she was related to Hernando Cortés to be romantic. Even more romantic is to know that Grandpa M.C.'s grandmother had two daughters during an on-going affair with a French trapper whom she never married. One of those daughters was Grandpa's mother, making my great-great-grandfather on my grandfather's side a visiting French trapper! With the Martinez, the Cortez, the French trapper, and the confluence of the cultures, there is a fair mixture in my grandparents "pure" genetic inheritance.

*Chapter 5*

# SUMMER AND WINTER MANSIONS

T he second wave of industrial growth picked up steam in the late nineteenth century, eventually spreading from eastern commercial centers to the territories along the railroad lines. Block ice refrigeration, wire communication, and the introduction of train transportation altered the American way of life. Factories and assembly lines started to produce mass quantities of textiles, clothing, packaged meats, and pressure-sealed cans. And laborers were needed for steel production, coal mining, and oil utilization, as well as the building of railroads and steamships.

As a result, millions of immigrants seeking a better life flooded the eastern part of the United States. Eager to feed their families, they were a cheap and plentiful workforce for the factories and mills. Sixty-hour work-weeks, unregulated employment conditions, harsh, demanding, and at times dangerous work areas, were tolerated by people anxious to keep their jobs. Employers had total power. And laws did not exist to protect the employees. Eventually, the fallout from employers' unregulated freedom to value productivity over human rights forced our government leaders to institute laws to protect the working populace.

Theoretically, in a free monopoly, especially before antitrust laws, anyone could become wealthy. A few did. It is said that in his later years, Andrew Carnegie earned one million dollars a month from his enterprises, while a factory steel mill worker in his employ earned only four dollars.

The few who achieved unbelievable wealth demonstrated their social positions by building extraordinarily large mansions. The grandeur of these mansions cannot be exaggerated: swimming pools, public-sized galleries, as many as one hundred rooms, plus thirty or more bathrooms.

Topiary gardens, with handcrafted marble walkways, led the guests past waterfalls, remarkable statues, and impressive flower gardens with strategically arranged seating areas under vine-covered arches.

These affluent families travelled between summer and winter mansions and hosted fabulous parties. With enough servants to pamper their overnight guests, they provided exotic foods, elaborate entertainment, and band music for ballroom dancing. They also travelled in luxury to foreign countries while collecting priceless artifacts and accumulating paintings by renowned artists. A lifestyle of lavish extravagance was their signature.

Ambitious capitalists, with their ability to build enterprising monopolies, set America on course to become a leader in the industrialized world. A coin has two sides, though. They were also America's first philanthropists, giving generously to the arts, culture, and education.

Northern New Mexico, during that time, however, was still the "Wild West." As the Gilded Age was coming to a close in the East, prospectors and moneyed entrepreneurs were attracted to the potential for great wealth and political power in the new territory. One of those entrepreneurs was

French chef, Henri Lambert. Once the personal chef to President Lincoln, Mr. Lambert, and his wife Mary, settled in Cimarron, New Mexico, where they had their first child. In 1872 they built the St. James Hotel on the main road through town. The hotel restaurant provided elegant dinners to the elite and many of the "Wild West" characters, such as Wyatt Earp, Bat Masterson, Black Jack Ketchum, members of the Santa Fe Ring, and countless other vigilantes, miners, and trappers. It is also believed that Little Annie Oakley visited the hotel while travelling with Buffalo Bill's Wild West Show.

Following the untimely death of their first son, Mary became pregnant again. On a cold stormy day in 1887, Mary Lambert gave birth in Room #31 of the hotel to a second baby boy. Henri and Mary were elated. Right from the beginning, Fred Lambert was destined to make history, because his parents asked a guest, Buffalo Bill Cody, to be his godfather.

At the tender age of sixteen, Fred became the youngest Territorial Marshal in New Mexico history. He continued an active role in law enforcement, wrote poetry, was a published author, and made several pen-and-ink drawings.

Fred also helped his parents maintain the St. James Hotel. When Fred replaced the roof, he found that the first-floor ceiling had been double reinforced to stop bullets from penetrating the upstairs rooms. It was the era of both hostile and friendly Indians, drunken cowboys, horse thieves, and cattle rustlers. And over 400 bullet holes were found in the ceiling.

By some accounts, as many as twenty-six people died in the hotel during the wild and raucous early days of the establishment. T.J. Wright checked in for the last time on March 31, 1882. He was shot as he left the gambling room—a gambling deal gone wrong—and stumbled back to Room #18 where he died.

His ghost apparently still haunts the hotel. The unexplained lingering smell of cigar smoke tells you T.J. is around. One woman claims she was mocking the ghost of T.J. when she felt two hands push her over the banister. Due to that and other such strange and tormenting events, Room #18 remains locked to the public.

Room #17 was Mary's room. The scent of her perfume lets you know she is around. Some say she cannot move on to the next stage because her firstborn son, who died tragically at the age of two, doesn't know he has died and continues to play in the hotel.

New Mexico, at the time, was being considered for acceptance into the Union. As the territory became more populated, the established non-English speaking people were displaced. It was feared that the language barrier would cause discrimination and prevent some children from receiving an equal education. School attendance was not mandatory. In poorer families education was sacrificed so children could help on the farm or care for younger siblings. My mother was lucky to have attended five years of elementary school in an English-speaking school in Taos. My father, meanwhile, had only three years of primary education at a Spanish-speaking school in Peñasco. Child labor laws were not yet in existence, but the political environment of New Mexico was changing rapidly.

**The Beautiful Springer Mansion
(Image courtesy of Chase Ranch Museum,
Cimarron, NM)**

**Mary Springer (on right) and possibly
Charles Springer in front seat of the Rolls Royce.
(Image courtesy of Chase Ranch Museum,
Cimarron, NM)**

*Chapter 6*

# THE ROSE GARDEN

Among the delegates attending the 1910 New Mexico Constitutional Convention was the fabulously wealthy lawyer, Charles Springer, brother of the renowned attorney, Frank Springer. Working from his office in Colfax County, Charles Springer amassed a fortune from cattle ranching and negotiating multiple lawsuits pertaining to the Maxwell Land Grant. Controversies over land ownership for railroad development, gold, coal, copper mining rights, and settlers' disputes, all required the representation of an attorney.

Mother remembered hearing that Charles Springer and his first wife, Lottie Chase, would take evening walks. Charles carried Lottie's little sister, Mary, piggyback.

In 1893, Lottie gave birth to a little girl who lived only a few days. Sadly, weakened by the baby's birth and death, Lottie died the following summer. Six years later, on November 30th, Charles Springer married twenty-two-year-old Mary Lorraine Chase, Lottie's younger sister.

Mary and Lottie Chase were born into a wealthy ranching family. As pioneers, her parents, Manly and Theresa Chase, had come from Wisconsin and crossed the Raton Pass on a covered wagon to settle in the New Mexico Territory. In 1867, they purchased 11,000 acres from Lucien Maxwell and established their ranching enterprise on land occupied by Ute and Apache Indian people. The couple brought in sheep, Texas Longhorn and Corriente cattle, and planted vast apple orchards. But they were in constant fear of Indian raids from the displaced people.

In 1901, Mr. Springer and his new wife, Mary, built their magnificent three-story mansion on the Chase Ranch near Cimarron. They hired skilled craftsmen and imported materials and textiles for the construction. When completed, an elite assemblage of adventurous wealthy people, renowned actors, and local politicians socialized there as guests of Mr. and Mrs. Springer, epitomizing the end of the Gilded Age. I am told that while visiting the Springers, Mary Martin, the original actress in *Peter Pan*, and other actors, performed on a scenic open space pavilion on the Vermejo Ranch, near Raton.

In their prime, Charles and Mary lived the life of the privileged few. When travelling to Philadelphia on shopping sprees, Mary Springer hired an entire train to accommodate her entourage of household servants. While in Philadelphia she entertained guests, attended social functions, allowed herself time for voice lessons, and spent hours shopping for eclectic furnishings and paintings to bring home to the mansion.

The Springer Ranch, like most ranches, did not have close neighbors, though Mrs. Springer had visitors who came by carriage. Mr. Springer was much older than his wife and, for the most part, occupied his time with his political involvement and law practice. The young, beautiful, and vivacious Mrs. Springer was always busy managing the household staff, travelling, and preparing for gala affairs.

One day a tall, handsome young man came to the Springer Mansion. After dismounting from his horse, he walked up the steps to the impressive entrance, slapped the dust off his pants, and removed his hat. He loudly rapped the brass knocker. A maid opened the door and stood silently looking at the tall, Spanish youth.

*"¿Esta La Señora Springer?"* he asked.

An elegant lady standing a few feet behind the maid stepped forward.

*"Soy La Señora Springer,"* she arrogantly responded. *"¿Que necesitas?"*

Continuing in Spanish, the tall youth said, "I have a message for you."

"Who are you?" she asked. Her eyes scanned the rugged young man standing before her.

*"Jose Ildefonso Sandoval, Senora Springer,"* he answered formally. "You've been expecting my cousin, Diego. We came from Peñasco, but Diego got sick on our way. I left him at the St. James Hotel." Stepping away from the door and putting his hat on to leave he added, "Diego should be here in a few days."

Mrs. Springer walked out onto the veranda. Elevating her voice, she further pursued the conversation. "What do you know about planting a rose garden, Jose?"

"How many acres do you have in mind?" he joked, looking across the vast acreage.

Mrs. Springer smiled, "You must be thirsty. You'll find the well around back." She directed him to the path leading around the mansion. "I'll meet you there to show you where I would like my rose bushes planted." She closed the door.

Mary Springer, according to my dad's story, took an immediate liking to him and hired him on the spot. Dad's cousin would never be hired at the ranch. It is no wonder she was intrigued with my father. He was a tall, good-looking man with light sandy-brown hair and striking hazel eyes. But it was something about his quiet, confident mannerisms that caught women off guard.

A couple of years later, Mother, at the age of thirteen, was sent to work at the Springer Mansion. Charles and Mary Springer were childless and raised their two young nieces, Gladys and Marjery England, after their mother died. On one of her many trips to Philadelphia, Mrs. Springer took my mother along to keep the young girls company. Mother would nostalgically describe the trip she took as part of the entourage to Philadelphia.

"The coal smoke from the train coated our skin and clothing," Mother said, detailing the long, tiresome journey to "Philly." She continued by describing the lavish accommodations they occupied once there. The affinity Mr. and Mrs. Springer had for Mother allowed her to be privy to many of their activities. When the Springers entertained, whether in Philadelphia or at the mansion, it was customary for my mother to bring the prettily dressed girls into the ballroom to formally greet the guests before bedtime.

Charles and Mary would take Mother, along with Gladys and Marjery, to the yearly Fourth of July celebration in Cimarron. Mother remembered Mrs. Springer supervising the decorating of their buggy. Bells were strapped to the horse's back and red, white, and blue ribbons streamed from the buggy in the breeze. Mr. Springer guided their horse-drawn entry into the parade line where participants all vied for ribbons or recognition.

After the parade, everyone gathered to watch the rodeo: bull and bronco riding, calf roping, barrel racing, and mutt and buck riding. My cousins, Freddy and Lee Cortez, competed in bull and bronco riding. We like to brag that Freddy, after so many years of winning, quit so others would have a chance. Mother said they won a lot of money and first place buckles which showed off their ranching skills.

After the rodeo's barbeque and barn dance, the Springer family and Mother would return to the mansion, where Mrs. Springer would ask, "Lenore, sweetheart, please give the girls a bath before putting them to bed."

Mother never saw a paycheck. Grandmother Gertrudes would ask a relative to take her from the Moreno Cimarron lumber camp, where they were living at the time, to the mansion to pick up Mother's monthly wages. At one time, Mr. and Mrs. Springer petitioned my grandparents to let them adopt my mother, but my grandparents respectfully denied their request.

Mother said she used to daydream about being a fashionable young lady who lived with her family in the beautiful Springer Mansion. She would pretend that the young cowboy, who her father had chased off years before, would come back to the mansion and ask her father for her hand.

Mother continued with her story. "I would imagine him telling my father that he and I were in love and, with or without his blessing, he was taking me to live with him at his large ranch house." She laughed. "Sometimes, I would imagine meeting him secretly by the pump house. He would take my hand, and we would walk along the creek. Then he would turn to me, as handsome as can be, put his hand under my chin, and kiss me. And, of course, in my imagination, the cowboy and I would live happily ever after."

When the roses were in bloom at the mansion, Mrs. Springer always asked Mother to cut fresh roses from the garden to keep the beautiful crystal vases throughout the house brimming with color. Mother, a petite girl with thick, curly black hair separated into long braids, would energetically go to the garden, shears in hand. After coming from the bunkhouse and heading out to the field, Dad would ride past the mansion and grin as he saw the radiant young girl in the garden pricking her fingers as she struggled to clip the thorny-stemmed flowers.

Once, Dad rode his horse up to her. "You're going to be bleeding all over the place before you have enough flowers to fill your basket."

He dismounted and took the shears from Mother's thorn-pricked hands to show her how to hold the branches and where to cut. When Dad's hand brushed across hers, she said she felt an odd surge through her body. Embarrassed, she wanted nothing more than for him to leave her alone. And uncomfortable with his standing so near, she pulled away from him. After cutting a couple of branches my dad handed the shears to her, encouraging her to follow his instructions. That was the beginning of a romance that would culminate in a lifetime of love, loss, and hardship.

Before then, though, Dad had been romancing Eva, a young woman who frequently visited the ranch. Nevertheless, Mother and Eva would become good friends and remain in contact for years.

One of the few errands Mother found disagreeable was when Mrs. Springer sent her to the field to ask "Fonzie," Mrs. Springer's nickname for my dad, to return to the mansion. Mrs. Springer would want him to do some menial work the yardmen could have easily done.

The field where Dad and the men were working one day was a lengthy walk. Mother arrived hot, sweaty, and short of breath. Dad grabbed hold of the reins on his horse, annoyed by the interruption and Mrs. Springer's request. He stepped up onto the saddle and reached his hand out to Mother, offering her to ride with him back to the mansion. Embarrassed, and somewhat confused by conflicting feelings, she refused his offer and started running back to the mansion. Dad curbed his horse to stay by her side, taunting her for being so foolish. She continued to run. He spurred his horse into a gallop and rode on to the mansion, turning to tip his hat in her direction. Years later, as

Mother relayed this story to me, Dad interrupted her to tell me that Mother was not only foolish but also headstrong.

Whenever Mary Springer was travelling, Charles Springer would take the opportunity to go hunting. "J.I. and I can manage on our own," Charles would tell Mary when she offered to leave some of the staff with him.

Dad would accompany Mr. Springer, setting up the camp, scouting for game, cooking, and caring for the horses. One year, for the Thanksgiving dinner, Dad went out a couple of nights before to scout for signs of roosting wild turkeys. Early on Thanksgiving Day, Dad led Mr. Springer to the feeding flock, and they returned with their Thanksgiving game.

Mutual respect created a bond between these two men of vastly different cultures. Mr. Springer treated my dad like a son. And according to what my brother, Ernest, remembers hearing, Dad was the only employee who had keys to the wine cellar.

During his work periods at the Springer Mansion, Dad wore many hats. One of the hats that he preferred *not* to wear was that of the chauffeur. Mr. Springer owned one of the first motorcars in Colfax County, a Rolls Royce, freighted in by train. One time, for some unknown reason, the chauffeur,

Tommy Sutcliffe, was not available. Mrs. Springer sent Dad, against his will, to a two-week school in Raton to learn how to drive. The school included lessons on how to repair the automobile.

But after only a few days away at school, Dad returned to the ranch, ready to drive the car during the chauffeur's absence. Baffled, Mrs. Springer asked him why he had not stayed to finish the training.

Glaring directly at her he responded gruffly, "I learned all that I need to know to drive and fix the car. I have better things to do with my time here at the ranch." Dad never was one for taking direction—especially from a woman.

My dad told me that sometimes at the end of the day, he would ride his horse over to the St. James Hotel on Main Street in Cimarron to meet his buddies for a drink or two in the bar. Just for fun one day, after having had a few too many drinks, Dad rode his horse, pistol in hand, into the St. James Saloon and fired bullets into the ceiling. Moments later he rode out the back door and knocked over the rain barrel in his haste.

Fred Lambert ran out the saloon's front door, grabbed the reins of his saddled horse from the hitching post and pursued my dad shooting into the air to make him stop. Mr. Springer offered to represent my dad in court after an angry Lambert initiated a lawsuit. Dad declined the offer and won the suit by claiming, "You can't stop a horse running from gunfire." Twenty-two gunshot holes, some of which may be from my father's gun, can still be counted in the ceiling of the bar.

Dad was not always a gun-slinging cowboy. At winter gatherings, ice-skating was one of the pleasures Mrs. Springer provided for her guests. Dad would take Mrs. Springer and her guests by buggy through the glistening snow over to the frozen pond, help her guests with their skates, and give the beginners instructions. He was never successful, however, in teaching Mrs. Springer to gracefully glide on ice.

"Her feet and mouth cannot work at the same time," he used to say, adding that she didn't concentrate and had a difficult time being silent. Each time she fell, her heavy long coat made it difficult for her to stand back up. With much ado, Mrs. Springer would call Dad for help. Dad would skate over to Mrs. Springer, a little annoyed, and lift her back onto her skates. She would beam with delight, holding onto his arm, thanking him profusely, which further annoyed Dad.

Dad quit the Springer Ranch on several occasions. One time, Mrs. Springer had asked Dad to stop the yard crew from their work and direct them to gather small pebbles from anthills to use as part of the landscape. Dad refused. She insisted. He quit.

She yelled. "Don't ever come back, Fonzie!"

"Don't need to worry about that, Mrs. Springer!" Dad yelled back.

Eventually, they reconciled. And my dad returned to the ranch. Mother told me that yelling matches between Dad and Mrs. Springer were frequent and could be heard throughout the mansion. With a wry smile, Mother said, "Even people in Cimarron could hear them yelling."

During one of the times Dad was not working for the Springers, someone burned down their barn. At that time, setting houses or barns on fire was a plague that affected all the ranchers. They were wary of the fires, knowing they were a sure way of getting revenge.

If fires were not caught early enough the entire structure would go up in flames. Buckets of water, filled from the pump house and passed along a human chain, were insufficient to drown a full-blown fire.

The guilty party was never identified. It was suspected that the fire had been set by either a vagrant sleeping in the barn trying to stay warm or a disgruntled landowner angry with Charles

Springer for representing a land right dispute in which the landowner lost his land. People said that if Dad had been working there at the time, the fire would not have happened because he had stopped past fires from causing serious damage.

Another time when Dad and Mrs. Springer had a quarrel, Charles and his brother, Frank, hired Dad to join the crew working on the completion of the Eagle Nest Dam. The dam was built in the beautiful Moreno Valley between Baldy Mountain and Wheeler Peak. Storing water from the Cimarron River, it supplied the water for the towns of Eagle Nest, Raton, and Springer, and the nearby ranches and farms. Amid pine, aspen, wildflowers, clean air, and a plethora of wildlife, the lake created by the dam became a haven for sportsmen. It was also a source for block-ice collection, a luxury before refrigeration.

As for my mother, working for Mr. and Mrs. Springer provided many new opportunities. She heard all the new songs, learned the newest dance steps, and saw the latest in women's fashion. This lavish lifestyle equipped her with new mannerisms, which enabled her to gain confidence and grace.

My father became enchanted by my mother's developing personality, and Mother enjoyed the attention he was giving her. They saw each other in the best of circumstances in the enlightened progressive environment. My father was learning a trade there; my mother was evolving into a new person. She was happy and comfortable and had it been her choice, I don't think she would have ever moved away.

By the time she turned nineteen, Mother and Dad had become very close. Dad proposed, and they decided to marry in the Taos Catholic Church. Relatives and friends all gathered in the reception hall to celebrate with the newlyweds as they were introduced.

*"Damas y Caballeros les presento Don Jose Ildefonso Sandoval y su esposa Lenore."* Following the dinner, the festivities began with the "Wedding March." Couples clasped and raised their hands to create a bridge as the new couple walked hand-in-hand under the arch, which signified the beginning of their new life together. Mother and Dad spent their wedding night in Grandmother's house. They left early the following morning to return to the Springer Mansion. Mother's younger brothers and sisters clung to her skirt, begging her to take them with her.

Mrs. Springer planned to have a small house built for the newlywed couple in the same style as the mansion. As construction began, Dad was called to serve in World War I. He left the Springer Ranch to serve his country.

Mrs. Springer pleaded with him to let my mother stay at the mansion until his return. "Lenore is happy here, Fonzie. Leave her here with me while you are away!"

But Dad knew the influence Mrs. Springer had over his wife. He did not argue, but promptly moved his reluctant, pregnant wife from the lavish, thriving environment to his small, rural family home in Peñasco.

# Chapter 7

# PEÑASCO

S imilar to my mother's family, my father's cultural and genetic inheritance is also influenced by the Spaniards. As Spain gained more and more land in the Americas, Spaniards began travelling north to the newly conquered land. A story handed down in my family tells us that in the late 1700s, a family travelling from Spain to visit New Spain was possibly as far as the Rio Grande when their twin sons were kidnapped by a native tribe. According to indigenous religious ideology, twins were a taboo that desecrated the land.

They were to be sacrificed to appease the feathered or the horned serpent. However, the tribal woman in charge of preparations for the sacrifice apparently allowed her compassion for the frightened fair-skinned Spanish boys to overcome her religious convictions. She devised an elaborate ruse that would convince her leaders the boys had escaped without her help, and hoped she would not be punished when they were discovered missing. She directed them north to what would later become the annexed part of Mexico—the New Mexico Territory.

The fate of one boy is unknown. The other boy is believed to have settled near Peñasco and is said to be my father's great-great-grandfather!

Located near the Picuris Indian Pueblo, some 20 miles south of Taos, is the small Spanish farming community of Peñasco. Few people moved there and fewer people moved away. Dad's mother, Andreita Pacheco, was born in Peñasco. She and her sister Frances were orphaned at a young age. No one offered to adopt the girls. They were shuffled from household to household as servants. They were subjected to the demands of people they didn't know and required to do whatever was requested of them.

Desperate to escape her plight, Grandmother Andreita, at a very young age, married the first man who proposed. My fraternal grandparents, Jose Emilio Sandoval and Andreita Maria Pacheco, were kind and content and did not embrace change. But Grandfather Jose Emilio was unhealthy. Dad remembers carrying him down to the river and propping him up in a chair so the frail man could watch his son fish.

Dad was only thirteen when his father died, leaving him the head of the family. In contrast to my mother's prodigious family, Dad had only one brother, Macedonio, and a sister, Frances, who was named after her mother's orphaned sister. All that is known of Dad's sister Frances is that she was very young when she slipped climbing a tree and died from her injuries.

Dad took on the responsibilities of his father but he was not prepared for the challenges he would face. Drinking was his escape. Dad became an alcoholic before he was a man. As an altar boy, he accompanied the priest and a church volunteer on their monthly trips from Peñasco to Santa Fe where they bought pure grape wine that would later be blessed and used during the Mass.

On those trips, they would all drink some of the wine, sipping to refresh themselves during their lunch. And it wasn't just at church. Dad was sent to buy alcohol for one of his aunts whenever the small bottle she carried in her apron pocket needed replacing. At a time when there were no liquor laws, it was fortunate that Dad had been hired on at the Springer Mansion, which took him away from an environment that encouraged his drinking.

When Mother arrived in Peñasco, Dad's widowed mother, Andreita; his brother, Macedonio; his wife, Delphinia; and their three children, welcomed my mother into their home, proud to fulfill my dad's request. Leaving the comfort of the Springer Mansion to live in this congested environment broke my mother's heart. Lonely, pregnant, and displaced, my mother involved herself with her husband's family accepting the changes she had to endure. She sewed for the women, mended worn garments, and introduced new recipes. She endeared herself to them, making the situation an acceptable, peaceful, productive relationship.

Soon after her arrival in Peñasco, Mother gave birth to her first child, a baby boy Dad would never know. Dad was away in the Army for just under two years. By the time he returned, baby Jose Emilio, named after his deceased Grandfather, had died from influenza during the pandemic of 1918-

1919, which killed an estimated fifty million people worldwide.

When Dad's military service ended, my parents returned to work for Charles and Mary Springer. Dad and Mrs. Springer's contentious relationship renewed and soon after his return, Dad and Mrs. Springer had an irreversible disagreement. My hot-tempered dad quit for the last time. Dad and Mother moved to Taos. Their anticipated house being built on the ranch was never completed.

**J.I. was away at war when Lenore gave birth to their firstborn child.**

**Baby Jose Emilio with Lenore.**

*Chapter 8*

# MY LITTLE VILLAGE

M other was determined to ignore the pain in her heart when she and Dad left the Springer Mansion for the last time. But, Mother's family greeted their sister and her husband with hugs and kisses when they arrived in Taos, insisting everyone sit down to eat. After dinner, the family helped Mother and Dad move their belongings into the small house they had rented just off the Plaza. It was the roaring twenties, and Mother and Dad quickly found work.

On April 12, 1924, news arrived in Taos that there had been a fire at the Springer Mansion. The ballroom on the third floor had gone up in flames, and the fire rapidly spread, destroying most everything of value in its wrath. Townspeople rushed to the scene and were able to save some of the furnishings, but they were unable to stop the fire. The beautiful mansion burned to the ground. The locals speculated that faulty electrical wiring caused the fire. Mother and Dad were devastated by the news. Fortunately, Charles and Mary were travelling at the time.

**The Springer Mansion (After the fire)**
**(Image courtesy of Chase Ranch Museum,**
**Cimarron, NM)**

Taos had changed from the days when Mother was a little girl. In 1898, two years after my mother's birth, two young American artists, Ernest Blumenschein and Bert Phillips, having met in Paris, returned to America with ambitious plans to travel to Mexico to paint. When they were forced to stop in Taos to repair their wagon wheel, the beauty of the area inspired them. They ended their journey there, settling in Taos. It was the beginning of the art movement. The wave of artists who settled in the area brought new attitudes and added new cultural tension, exasperating the already existing presumed distinction of hierarchy among the cultures.

To the artists and entrepreneurs coming to the new territory from the eastern United States, the sun-dried mud brick homes of the area embodied everything sacred and natural. They felt that to live within the cool walls of the adobe earthiness imparted a sense of spiritualism. Intrigued with the clothing and exotic features of the Tiwa Indian, and the colorful Spanish festivals and tempting food, these new residents enthusiastically encouraged their friends to visit. Many of those visitors also stayed.

From far and wide, the artisans with their brushes and chisels, and the authors and poets with their pens, fell in love with the unique assembly of cultures in the beautiful place of my heritage. They brought their wealth and their ways and stayed to paint, sculpt, write, and change the course of my little village. How differently my birthplace would have evolved had the artists not fallen in love with the area.

Grandmother Gertrudes emphatically believed that the cultures should remain separate. At first the long-time Spanish residents in Taos were too shy or too rebellious to learn the English language. And to my knowledge, few ever learned to fluently speak the local Tiwa language. The Anglo's affluence and easy confidence was a threat to their established ways. Long-time residents complained that the newcomers took too many liberties and were too free in what the local people reasoned was not their territory, their land, or their village.

Mother tells me that the only time the different cultures in Taos came close to socializing together was at the yearly Spanish fiesta honoring Santa Ana and Santiago. The fiesta played a major social and religious role in the lives of the Taos residents. During this gala, people from the different cultures dropped their biased guard and celebrated. The newcomers mingled freely, as the

Indian men and women, proud and stoic in their native attire, stood separately, watching as the Spaniards began their religious procession.

I know Mother and Dad attended the fiesta every year. Even years later, after I was born, Mother would take all of us to the fiesta. I vaguely recall the chaos following the Mass, as everyone scrambled to find their places in line. Each year the ceremony was the same. With an altar boy at his side, the priest, holding a thurible, led the procession. Other altar boys in their white cassocks followed carrying long crosses close to their chests. Next in line came six men hoisting a platform supporting a statue of Santa Ana. Then came other men displaying colorful, symbolic religious banners. A long line of Catholic towns-people, some holding lit candles, completed the procession. Along the way, the priest blessed the people with incense smoke from the thurible, and people chanted prayers. The procession left the church and paraded around the plaza before returning to the church grounds. Once the solemn religious obligations were fulfilled, the festivities began.

People travelled miles from other towns, villages, and pueblos to participate. Indian, Spanish, and English-speaking people all crowded into the plaza. All were confident to represent their dissimilar cultures through their languages, mannerisms, clothing and traditions, and in unity, enjoyed the occasion. Fiesta was a time for eating, drinking, flirting, and visiting with old friends. Some who attended were content to sit back and watch. Occasionally, overindulgence provoked a fistfight, and for some, ruined their day.

Mother found offensive the inability of the local people to accept cultural differences, as well as their inclination to feel threatened by new attitudes. She was not a crusader for the oppressed, did not impose her convictions on others, nor did she submit to the confinement placed on her by culture, race, or religion. She saw humanity on the same level, with each person possessing his or her own unique purpose.

Mother was equally comfortable associating with her relatives and Spanish friends as she was with her artist and Indian friends. Many of the now-prominent artists were my family's neighbors. Mother shared our Spanish food and culture with them. And they shared their artistic talent and cosmopolitan wisdom with her. She would sew and alter clothing for the artists. She appreciated their enlightened ways.

I don't think Mother consciously acknowledged the notion that she was broaching a new frontier of integration without government intervention. Many in the village of Taos, however, were critical of her unbiased attitude. They admonished her for putting on airs by associating with the artists and perplexed by her easy association with the Indian people. Entrenched in their Spanish heritage, my relatives contended that assimilation would bring about disintegration of their language, their religion, and their ways.

By the time my sisters, Bea and Carolyn, and my brothers, Ernest and Tony, were born, my mother had become well acquainted with the artists who lived nearby. Neighbor Bert Phillips, years after stopping to fix his broken wagon wheel, influenced my siblings' appreciation of art. Mr. Phillips watched how hard my mother worked to take care of her family. As a good neighbor he helped her by taking Bea and Carolyn on his painting field trips. Mr. Phillips allowed them to use his paint palette to paint on scraps of lumber left over from my father's carpenter jobs. It was an added bonus for my sisters that on the way to the site, Mr. Phillips would stop at the mercantile and buy a nickel bag of candy to share with them as they painted.

The little girls freshly bathed and wearing pretty homemade dresses smartly starched, gleefully left with Mr. Phillips. Mother's friends chastised her for letting them go with a foreigner. But whenever her little daughters, about five and seven years old, were gone for a few hours, Mother had time to care for her younger sons.

Ruphina, a woman who occasionally came from the Taos Pueblo to help my mother with her younger children and domestic chores, was the recipient of my mother's unbiased treatment.

One day as Ruphina helped four-year-old Ernest with his shoes, she turned to Mother. She brought Ernest close to her and pressed her cheek to his. In limited Spanish she pleaded, "Lenore, me have Ernest? Love him much. Want him as my own."

After hearing Ruphina's impassioned words, Mother hugged her. Taking both of Ruphina's hands, Mother said, "You make me happy to love my son so much. He loves you and would be happy with you, but he belongs here with his family."

Many times when Grandmother Gertrudes summoned my mother for help, Mother left Ernest and Tony with Ruphina. She would take her two young daughters and tread a path from her home in the middle of town near Pueblo Road to Grandmother's house on Martinez Lane. She would drop whatever she was doing to help her mother:

wash the heavy bedding, whitewash her walls, sew, or run an errand. My sisters found these visits unpleasant because Grandmother was not nice to them, nitpicking everything they did with constant reprimands.

One time when Grandmother wanted Mother to take her to the plaza to shop for fabric, she told Mother the girls could not go. Mother did not respond, so my sisters assumed they would also be going to town. As the women left my Grandmother's house, the girls followed a short distance behind. Grandmother became aware of them and bent down to pick up a handful of rocks. With unerring accuracy, she threw the rocks at them. She shook her finger at them and in a loud voice, warned them not to follow.

Years later, when my sister Carolyn told me this story, I asked her, "Was Grandmother purposely aiming the rocks at you to hurt you or was she just threatening you?"

Raising her eyebrows with wide-open eyes, Carolyn said, "Really aiming at us. And when we got hit two or three times we stopped following and went crying back to the house."

I could hear in her voice that the pain of the rejection still lingered. "What did Mother do? What did she say to Grandmother?" I asked.

"Nothing," my sister said indignantly. She told me that Mother accepted this atrocity to her daughters, knowing that to counter her mother's action would only add fuel to her rage. So, with a lump in her throat and a heavy heart, Mother endured the abuse in silence. No matter what sacrifice Mother made, her efforts were never sufficient to merit Grandmother Gertrudes' approval. My mother went through her entire life deliberately avoiding anger—never making a scene, never lashing out at the ones she loved, never purposely harming a soul.

I've attempted to decipher and limit the ambiguity between discipline and abuse. We may never come to terms with Grandmother's severe parenting, but we can understand her challenges and her passion to maintain control. My attempt to understand my mother's submissiveness, even as an adult, is ineffectual. I remain pained for my mother, my sisters, and my grandmother—conflicted between compassion and disapproval. I hesitate to judge. If their challenges had been mine to bear, I question what path *I* would have taken.

My sisters were not the only ones to learn from the artists. When my shy brother, Tony, was about the age of six, my mother noticed he had a natural inclination for art. He liked to carve horses from firewood. When he took one of his efforts to school, his teacher, Mrs. McGill, was so impressed she suggested he work with artist Ila Mae McAfee. Mother and Tony visited Mrs. McAfee's home, located a few houses from where my family lived. Together they set a time for his lessons.

After returning home, Mother excitedly said to my sister, "Carolyn, take Tony every day after school to the back door of Mrs. McAfee's home and wait there until he's ready to come home."

Carolyn gladly accepted, happy at the prospect of leaving the evening chores for Bea. Tony filled Mrs. McAfee's wood box, brought in water, and rendered other small chores in exchange for the art lessons. He learned her specialties: the basics of painting horses and the techniques of drawing the curvature of a dome.

Meanwhile my dad did odd carpenter jobs in between freighting to Peñasco and other small communities around Taos. In the evenings, Dad ducked his lanky figure under the doorway of the local bar to socialize.

My brothers tell me Dad loved Taos history. He frequently talked to them about the colorful characters of the West. Dad went all the way back to the days when his grandfather Jose Miguel

Sandoval and Great Grandpa Lucas Cortez occupied the same ground as many notable historic figures who were hardworking, business-minded adventurers on one hand, but advantageous, greedy—sometimes even murderous tricksters—on the other.

Dad told my brothers about Kit Carson who was a mountain man, Indian Agent and later an Army officer. He is remembered as a hero by some but a villain by others. Carson spoke English, Spanish, and many Indian languages but never learned to read. Under military obligation, Carson reluctantly followed orders to subdue the Navajo people and relocate them to isolated areas. Navajo men, women, and children were forced to walk 300 miles in 18 days, leaving behind their established ways and taking only the clothes on their backs. Many died under the harsh, barbaric conditions.

And then there was the story of the shocking scalping of Governor Charles Bent. Dad told the boys Governor Bent was hated by almost as many people as those who loved him. The once mountain man and trapper owned a number of wagon trains freighting on the Santa Fe Trail. In 1846, he was appointed the first civilian governor in the New Mexico Territory. During the 1847 Taos Rebellion, an uprising of Mexican and Pueblo people protesting the occupation of the United States, killed and scalped Bent in his home in Taos.

In 1880, the year Grandmother Gertrudes was born, the colorful entrepreneur, Long John Dunn, came to Taos. A reputed cattleman, saloonkeeper, jailbird, miner, and gambler, his lasting claim to fame was that he owned the only bridge over the Rio Grande that connected Taos to Embudo. And it was a lucrative toll bridge that charged for passengers, freight, and animal passage. Long John Dunn built a hotel in a canopy of riverside trees to accommodate the travelers. He kept a cow for fresh milk. Fish from the Rio Grande were cooked and served to the hotel guests. He also owned the first car in Taos and provided a taxi service, which gave him a transportation monopoly.

The respected town doctor, Thomas Paul Martin, better known as Doc Martin, was born in 1864, a few years before my grandfather M.C. Martinez was born. Doc Martin was a member of the New Mexico Medical Society. For a long time he was the only physician in Taos. Before buying one of the first cars in the area, he made house calls on horseback. As a Freemason and one of the first Shriners in New Mexico, he played an important role in the development of the village. His medical practice served the Pueblo Indians, Penitentes, Taos residents, and people in surrounding communities. Some say Doc Martin healed more bullet holes than illnesses.

I suppose the most controversial of my dad's stories is one about the secret society of Penitentes. The society originated in Spain and is still active in rural communities in New Mexico. Meetings are held in windowless, unadorned adobe buildings called *moradas*.

One simple cross is placed above the door and another on the roof. The main activities are held during Holy Week and involve fasting, self-flagellation, prayers, and carrying a rough-hewn, heavy cross, emulating Christ's suffering at His crucifixion.

Their practice is designed to expiate the sins of others through self-inflicted punishment. With extreme selflessness, the society adheres to a strict moral code, perpetuating the Catholic religion by caring for the sick, poor, and elderly. In remote villages of Spanish origin, where a priest is not in residence, the Penitente serves as spiritual leaders, performing some of the basic religious tasks for the community.

Taos is indeed unique. It is not really identifiable with any single individual ethnic group or country.

The abundant natural resources, the beauty, and the varied cultural backgrounds drew many outgoing, interesting characters from around the world. The Pueblo people, the Spaniards, the established Mexican settlers, the English-speaking newcomers, and the French trappers were all reticent to change. They tended to identify within their cultural parentage. Over time, however, this community developed a new culture of its own, a melting pot of the distinctly different ancestries. These are my forefathers.

*Chapter 9*

# A WEALTHY HEIRESS COMES TO TOWN

M y family often spoke of one particularly interesting newcomer. The wealthy heiress, Mabel Ganson Evans Dodge Sterne, had travelled to foreign countries and had entertained many now-famous artists, writers, and philosophers before moving to Taos. Mabel, who was living lavishly on an inheritance, wanted to escape from the disillusionment of her opulent existence. Arriving in Taos in 1917, she hoped to establish a new identity. Mabel encouraged the transplanting of many of her wealthy, enlightened friends and began a new social clique in an attempt to establish a new intellect in Taos.

The beauty of the landscape and the simple, unaffected values of the Indian people, who did not recognize personal material gain as achievements of social merit, helped Mabel heal her fragmented self-image. According to Mabel's memoir, *Edge of Taos Desert: An Escape to Reality,* Maurice, her husband at the time, had come to New Mexico before his wife and wrote to her from Santa Fe. He suggested she come to "save the Indians" and share their art and culture with the world.

Shortly after moving to Taos, Mabel asked Doc Martin about a place to rent. He suggested she speak to Mr. Manby, a well-known eccentric, who had a spacious house next to the doctor's office. The accommodations, not far from the Indian Pueblo, were perfect for her in her pursuit of developing a friendly relationship with the Indian people. During this time she became acquainted with Tony Luhan, an attractive Indian man from the pueblo.

As her relationship with Tony evolved, Mabel experienced a new liberation. Her mania for the Indian culture and Tony's complacent acceptance of her sealed their love. For the first time in her life, Mabel was recognized solely for herself, which enabled her to pursue her writing and love of art. She was free to indulge her secular passion for influencing society with new thinking, and she devoted time and energy to preserving the Indian way of life.

My family talked about Tony and Mabel, saying that Tony was married to a woman from his pueblo, but Mabel took great pleasure in identifying herself with him. Accordingly, she would have him wear his ceremonial feathered headdress and native attire to pose for pictures she shared with her friends. Tony would escort her to functions where she, with flare and pride, put him and their relationship on display.

Stories I have heard suggest that Mabel asked Tony to divorce his wife and marry her. In turn, she would be financially responsible for his family's welfare. The talk around town at the time was that Tony was in love with Mabel, but on occasion, would visit the pueblo to have conjugal visits with his ex-wife.

Many Spanish people of the village found Mabel abrasive and intrusive and her interracial marriage to Tony Luhan in 1923 absolutely shocking! To them, her behavior was unacceptable and fanned their already inflamed feelings about the mingling of these two cultures. Justifying their biased judgment with acerbic comments and condemnations, the people from the village prattled on about this social, racial, and religious irregularity for many years.

If Tony and Mabel took notice of the critical judgment of their union, it did not bother the couple. They and their wealthy friends—the town merchants, writers, and artists—did not concern themselves with the provincial opinions of the townspeople. The couple's friends relished the unusual combination of the two cultures elevating Mabel's position in her exclusive social clique still further.

After their marriage, Mabel and Tony built a large, luxurious adobe house on land they had purchased adjacent to the Taos Pueblo. Artist Georgia O'Keeffe, photographer Ansel Adams, and writers Mary Austin and D. H. Lawrence were among the many friends who enjoyed the comfortable environment and intellectual conversations encouraged by Mabel. For many years, Mabel's wealth, coupled with her unconstrained, distinctive cosmopolitan personality, was the core of this elite group in Taos.

Mother's nephew was a chauffeur for Mabel. He found Mabel domineering. She was the first person to receive commercial "curb service." She would call the bookstore, specify the books she was interested in, and set a time for her arrival. My cousin talked about how the clerk would carry the requested books to the curb, and within the comfort of her chauffeur-driven car, Mabel would make her selections. The native Taoseños were taken aback by her confident, forward manner. My mother was not. Mother identified with Mabel's quest for change and independence.

*Chapter 10*

# A MYSTERY IN TAOS

T he stories my family told me of the mysterious Mr. Arthur Rochford Manby have always piqued my interest. He lived in Taos with his dog, Lobo, down the road from where my parents lived. Early one morning, my dad walked with his dog, Shep, at his side past Mr. Manby's house on his way to the Taos Plaza. Frequently, Dad tipped his hat in greeting and occasionally stopped to visit with an acquaintance while the dog waited patiently.

Encountering the unfriendly Mr. Manby, Dad greeted him with a nod.

Mr. Manby, wearing an expensive worsted jacket, riding breeches and black riding boots, stopped my dad and firmly announced, "I want to buy your dog—price will not be an issue."

Shep, a longhaired, fawn-colored companion resembling the Catalan Sheepdog, had been in the family since he was a puppy. Shep walked with my sisters to school in the morning and knew when to return to the school to walk them back home. With only one or two words, Dad would instruct Shep to keep other animals away from the beef jerky drying on an outdoor rack. When Dad freighted, he trained his shaggy mixed-breed companion to protect the wagon and team of horses in his absence. He was a smart, happy, tail-wagging dog, and all the neighbors loved him.

Looking down at his dog, Dad responded in equal firmness. "This is a family pet and not for sale."

The following morning, my sisters found their dog a few feet away from the house. Shep was nearly dead. My father gently picked up the limp dog, wrapping him in a blanket. He followed Mother into the house. As she sat down in the rocking chair, he gently placed Shep on her lap where she rocked him until he died. Out in the yard, Dad dug a big hole where the family buried their loved pet, swathed in his blanket. During the night the family pet had been poisoned.

Many years before, in 1883, Manby, at the age of twenty-four, came from England to make his fortune in the new territory. He got off the train and found himself in the then-frontier town of Raton. On the horizon in front of him was the boundlessness of the Sangre de Cristo Range, with its waves of pine trees, white bark column clusters of tall aspens, and vast open space. It was a panorama of wilderness and opportunity without end.

Shrewd and determined to acquire land, Manby studied maps, grants, and local land transactions while still living in Raton. By the time he had moved to Taos, the obsessive, enterprising newcomer had learned to ride Western style and shoot a pistol. He introduced himself to all the merchants, bankers, miners, saloonkeepers, and the cowpokes.

He rode his horse to the scattered homesteads to talk to struggling Mexicans living on land grants issued by the Mexican government. He questioned them about their financial situations, particularly about their land, with a covert intent to exploit them. Manby amassed large tracts of land in

Northern New Mexico by paying delinquent taxes and putting a lien on those properties. When the owners defaulted, Manby assumed ownership.

Manby would stop at nothing to get what he wanted. He solicited money from his family and friends, promising lucrative profits on their investments. He married twice, each time romancing young maidens in hopes of enticing their wealthy parents to invest in his ideas. With each marriage he had a child. One baby was stillborn; the other lived only a short time. Both marriages ended in divorce, and both families suffered large financial losses.

Manby offered to finance the Mystic Gold Mine venture with two partners: Mr. Wilkinson, who mysteriously disappeared, and Mr. Ferguson, who is rumored to have committed suicide in the Las Vegas insane asylum. Manby was then left as sole owner of the mine. On paper he plotted the creation of an oasis at the natural hot springs with hotel accommodations to attract the rich. Manby was confident he could develop a profitable business by making the Indian Pueblo a commercial tourist attraction. To his investors, he projected detailed plans of a restaurant and hotel, and how he would plant trees along the road leading to the pueblo. All of the financial participants invested enthusiastically. All lost their money.

By the 1900s, Manby had been in and out of trouble with the law for murder, unpaid debts, and questionable land transactions. His nefarious tactics were well known, and he was highly disliked in Taos and the surrounding communities. For years, he planned, cheated, tricked, begged, lied, and bribed to bring these claims to pass in his favor, never doubting that one day they would all be his. After finally toppling previous ownerships, the courts awarded vast tracts of land in Manby's favor. The inability, however, to find new investors and the stress of a lien on his estate on the main road in Taos drove Manby to worry, fear, and paranoia. He barricaded himself in his locked home and became a recluse living in filth, decaying both mentally and emotionally.

In 1929, the old recluse, Manby, had not been seen for many days. Concerned, but mostly curious, neighbors climbed over a wall to enter the house from the rear. After passing neglected lilac bushes and a barking dog tied to a pole, they entered the house. Thick dust covered every item. The entire place was in shambles. The kitchen counter was covered with dirty dishes and rotting food. Flies and a foul stench exacerbated the utter disarray. On a cot they found a fully clothed, swollen, and decomposed body, minus a head. Maggots and flies covered the exposed, decaying flesh. In an adjacent room, they found a skull bearing teeth marks.

Manby's harrowing demise reverberated throughout the town. Even posthumously, this most colorful figure continued to cause disgust, detest, and disbelief. The discovery of the decapitated corpse provoked a multitude of suppositions. One is that Manby had devised a ruse to gain a new identity and leave Taos to escape his creditors. It was speculated that he dug up the newly interred body of Mr. Brooks from the cemetery, took it to his house, decapitated the corpse and left it in his stead. Another supposition is that his dog attacked him and chewed off his head. And still another was that he was murdered. The mystery surrounding the demise or disappearance of this controversial figure has never been solved.

While the village was lit with gossip and suppositions over the mystery, another chapter of my mother and father's life was coming to a close. It was during this time that my sisters recall seeing my mother chasing my father around the rough-hewn pillars supporting the loft they used as their bedroom. Mother was trying to take a bottle of alcohol away from Dad. It was at the time of the stock market crash of 1929 and Dad had not worked for some time.

**Ernest, Raymond and Tony feeding the
cow at the Rayado Ranch.**

# Chapter 11

# THE CONVERTED
# TACK ROOM

Traveling west from Fort Leavenworth, the stagecoach crossed the Arkansas River and rumbled through the pine and aspen forest along the Santa Fe Trail. It stopped in the Northern New Mexico town of Rayado. Cutting through hunting and powwow grounds of nomadic Indian tribes, the stagecoach was under constant threat of Indian attack.

It was in 1848, that Lucien B. Maxwell established the town of Rayado on the eastern valley slopes, at the southern tip of the Sangre de Cristo Mountains. Lucien Maxwell persuaded Kit Carson to come live in the new ranching town to protect the people from threat of attack. A Federal garrison post was established in Rayado in 1850. During the Civil War, Rayado was an important supply stop for Colorado troops headed to Glorieta Pass.

Years later in 1922, Iowa-born Waite Phillips, having amassed great wealth in oil enterprising, purchased 300,000 acres from Maxwell, which included the established town of Rayado. On this land, he developed a highly-regarded ranch with polo ponies, fine workhorses, sheep, buffalo, and a cow and calf operation.

When the ranch grew enough and needed a foreman, an old unused tack room was converted into living quarters to accommodate the foreman and his family. Given the economic conditions following the stock market crash of 1929, my dad was fortunate to have been offered the position late that year. My family then moved from Taos to Rayado. A jack-of-all trades, Dad was also the occasional blacksmith and butcher on the ranch.

My brothers, sisters, and parents, plus occasional visitors, lived in the converted tack room. It was a long wooden building with dirt floors and three small rooms, each with a door facing the road. Furniture brought from Taos crowded the rooms. My brothers slept in one room on wooden bunks my dad had made. The next room was the living room, which became a bedroom for my sisters at night. The third room was the kitchen, with a little alcove where my parents slept. At night, they pulled the rollaway bed away from the wall, then folded it up and covered it during the day.

In this house, Mother cooked, cleaned, and sewed all the clothes her family wore. In the evening, Dad used his time to improve the tack room, repair the worn leather soles on their shoes, and build cabinets and furniture to make the tack room more livable. Dad made stilts, sleds, and other toys for my brothers and sisters.

On school days, my four older siblings walked a mile to wait for the bus to take them to the town of Miami, New Mexico. Looking smart wearing Mother's sewing efforts, they went off to school confident and prepared. My sister Carolyn told me that after school, they participated in snowball fights, "ice skating" on the frozen beaver pond, wearing shoes since they had no skates, and sledding on homemade contraptions. In the summertime they fished, rode horses, scouted, and swam in the pond.

The men who worked for Phillips brought their families, so there were many playmates with whom my brothers and sisters could share the freedom of childhood. On Saturday evenings, adults played cards at the kitchen table. The children made taffy or fudge loaded with piñons or performed a stage play for family members. On Sundays after attending mass, the parents, eager for a day of rest, absolved the children of chores, leaving them free to entertain themselves with quiet activities like hunting for arrowheads in the fields behind the house.

Now employed and drinking less, Dad's sober and naturally pleasant personality encouraged Mother to relax with their relationship. The two talked freely, making plans for the future. Sometimes they sat chatting while playing cards. Mother, interrupting their peaceful moments, tended to the food on the stove or checked on the children. My brothers and sisters said that the years lived in Rayado were some of the happiest times for the family.

It was during this same time that Dad's blind mother, Andreita, came from Peñasco to spend happy days with her grandchildren. Carolyn remembers that Dad secured a tight rope along the path to the outhouse so that Grandma Andreita could navigate from the kitchen door to the outhouse. Each time Grandma stayed with them, Mother tailored a new wardrobe for her.

When Mother became pregnant with me, she travelled to Taos to be with her mother for my birth. When we returned to Rayado, Dad, in anticipation of my arrival, had built a wooden cradle for me. Ten years older than I, Tony was knocked out of his pampered position as the youngest after I was born. I have been told that Tony felt hurt and resentment by the attention I received. His retaliation sometimes put me in danger.

One day Mother was hanging clothes on the line. "Tony, put Rosabelle in the stroller and take her for a walk," she said.

A hill led down from our house to a grassy clearing. Tony pushed my handmade stroller and sent me speeding dangerously down the hill. He laughed as I giggled all the way. When reprimanded, he told Mother, "She wanted to do it." Ernest tells me I loved it and begged to do it again.

I remember my brothers telling me that before I was born they often got into trouble. Sitting on the floor cross-legged with my teddy bear in my arms, I listened to every word as they dramatized the details of their antics and how Dad had punished them. Their stories made me grateful I was born naturally good—or so my mother always said.

They told me about the wild, nomadic burros that roamed freely on the ranch. Spaniards introduced burros to the New World during the 1500s. Through the years these wild donkeys, tough-as-nails, foraged the range, free to fend for themselves until rounded-up to be used as beasts of burden by miners, prospectors, and traders. For one reason or another, many burros were never caught. Some escaped their owners or outlived them.

Dad forbade my brothers from riding the wild burros, warning them about the danger. One day, my brothers' friend, Raymond, caught a wild burro, jumped on its back, and coaxed Tony to jump on behind him. Raymond first asked my brother Ernest to ride, but he refused. Raymond goaded Ernest, calling him chicken and from the burro's back he yelled, "I'll bet your little brother ain't too scared to ride with me."

Tony, who was about seven years old at the time, took the bait and tried several times to jump upon the burro's back. The wild animal moved around too much, and Tony was too short. "Climb the fence and jump on behind me," Raymond said, as he urged the burro closer.

Before Tony could use wise judgment he was straddling the burro, his arms tightly hugging his friend's waist. The animal ran headlong for all he was worth. Raymond saw the fast-approaching clothesline and lowered his head, calling back to Tony to do the same. Poor Tony did not hear him in time to duck his head, and the clothesline caught his throat, throwing him off the burro. Tony hit the ground hard. Crying loudly, he grabbed his shoulder and curled himself into a ball, swaying back and forth in agony.

Ernest ran to the blacksmith shop. "Dad, come quick! Tony is hurt."

Dad put down his hammer and doused the hot iron in a bucket of water. He took off his apron and followed my brother to the clearing where Tony was lying surrounded by sympathizers. He carefully picked Tony up in his arms and carried him into the house and placed him gently on the bed.

Tony lay very still submerging his pain, frightened and fearful of the consequences. Dad silently and methodically examined his shoulder. Feeling satisfied with his diagnosis, Dad put his foot against Tony's torso and took hold of Tony's left hand. He pulled steadily until the dislocated shoulder slipped back into place.

Dad then stood up, took his belt off and whipped Tony for not obeying him. My brother Ernest, two years older than Tony, was wiser and more fearful of Dad's punishments. Ernest did not ride the burro, but that didn't stop him from getting *his* whipping. Dad punished him with the same belt, but harder. Scolding Ernest, he told him that the extra punishment was because he was older and should have stopped his little brother from riding. Usually Tony was quick to stay out of Dad's angry path. He was able to con his way out of trouble by feigning sickness or blaming his siblings and escape the harsh treatment directed to my brother Ernest.

Dad was partial to his light-skinned children, which was rewarded by their fawning over him. Ernest's dark skin played against him. Honest and forthright, Ernest tried but never found a way to please Dad or escape his misdirected temper. Dad treated my sisters with the same erroneous partiality. My fair-skinned sister, Carolyn, was Dad's golden child. She could do no wrong. Carolyn learned early that she could get her way by siding with Dad. She was praised for not being like her independent big sister, and no one in the family stood up to her.

Talkative, impulsive, and artistically inclined, my sister Bea could do no right. Each time her efforts for independence were thwarted, she became more entrenched in her less-than-cooperative attitude. Mother would dress her daughters in smartly smocked, handmade dresses and fix their hair with pretty ribbons. Bea would chew on the smocking and pull the ribbons from her hair.

While Carolyn was making a "perfect child" example, Bea, asked to smile, would defiantly frown. Being placed in the back of the classroom, due to her disruptive nature, greatly emphasized Bea's poor, uncorrected eyesight. When Bea was a baby, Grandmother Andreita, with good intention, tied her little left arm behind her with a diaper in an effort to force her to use her right hand in the belief that being left handed was a bad omen that would cause her trouble throughout her life. As Bea grew older, her left hand was slapped any time she attempted to use it.

My dad may have been too harsh with his punishment and too strict and limiting, but in general, my mother was too lenient. If ever she could be judged for being partial to a certain child or person, it was because their need appeared overly apparent to her. By the time I was born,

Dad's control over the family had been greatly reduced by his drinking and by my mother's continual determination to improve our situation.

My sisters tell me that I was an unusually good baby and I would not allow them to pamper me. I can truly accept that I was a good baby and I understand why: I was born to a mostly absentee alcoholic father and a mother who gave me all the freedom in the world to make my own decisions. She supported me in all my actions. Lastly, I had four older brothers and sisters, and I was cuddled and loved like a puppy. Yes, I was born naturally good—good and lucky.

**Cousins Loyola and Eileen with
Rosabelle holding her Teddy Bear**

# Chapter 12

# LENORCITA

L atc in the year of 1937, my family of seven left Rayado and moved back to Taos. This time we lived in a three-room adobe house rented from my Aunt Pritz. I had a little tricycle and Mother would cut paper into confetti, placing the little pieces into a tin cup. She would throw the confetti high in the air in front of me. I would pedal as fast as my little legs could move and ride giggling through the festive paper shower. With a big smile on her face, Mother would clap her hands. And I would beam.

It was a rusty tricycle with a semi-solid steel frame and a raised platform on the back. Ernest would place one foot on the platform. With his hands on the handlebars he'd push me, racing as I called out, "faster, faster!" Sometimes I toted a playmate standing on the platform with her hands on my shoulders. We'd travel to imaginary places. The end of the fence was the Plaza. We pretended the front door of the house was the entrance to the mercantile. Other times, Mother tied a small cardboard box to the tricycle frame so I could pull my teddy bear.

La Loma, was settled in 1870 by the Spaniards. The houses were built in a circle and connected to each other to create an enclosure that would serve as a defense from Indian attack. When I lived there, the families in this cluster of six adobe homes shared the community water very much like they did when La Loma was first built. The yards were hard-packed dirt with hollyhock flowers and morning glories climbing the wire fences. Everyone gathered at the well to hear the gossip and share woes.

The well, located a few feet from our kitchen door, was our only water source. Each week Mother built a fire on the hard-packed dirt between the well and our house. She then placed a galvanized tub filled with water on the fire. Through the harsh winters and scorching hot summers, my mother washed her family's laundry on a washboard, using lye soap she had made herself. After the rinsing and the wringing, the clean wash was hung on a heavy-gauge wire strung between two poles. A long stick with a deep groove at one end was placed at the center of the wire. This was an important stick. It held the wash high off the ground. Should the wind or an errant child dislodge this stick, the wet clothing would fall and become muddied and need rewashing.

Life was harsh and demanding for my mother, but not for me. Tony was, for the most part, a good big brother. But he loved to tease me. He would throw my teddy bear up in the air and sock it hard as it came down, whispering, "This is you."

I would cry out and Mother would come to my aid. "Tony, what are you doing to her?"

"I'm not even touching her," Tony would answer, affecting a shocked look and raising his arms up in bewilderment.

Our home, warmed by the big black kitchen stove, my mother's endless, selfless activities and a regularly rotating barrage of visiting friends and relatives, provided a continuously happy, nurturing life for me. It is in this humble setting, when I was still quite young, that I have a disturbing memory.

From the small middle room, used as a bedroom at night and a living room by day, I remember seeing my mother lying in a bed in the bedroom. The foot of the bed had been elevated with blocks and a small bucket placed under the thin, blood-saturated mattress. If I close my eyes, I can still hear the plink of the drops as the blood hit the bucket.

*The little house is filled with unfamiliar activity. The usual loud camaraderie is replaced with soft-stepping women speaking in whispers. They rush in and out of the hot, steamy kitchen, to the yard, or in and out of my mother's room. In a no-nonsense tone I am told to be quiet and to stay out of the way. Intensely lonely, desperately in need of comforting, I focus my sight on my mother's face. I want to be soothed by her touch. I need her assurance that whatever is wrong will soon be right and that the warm, cheerful atmosphere she provides will be back in place. But everyone in this little house is too busy to sense my anxiety. In this middle room I sit quietly, invisible to my family and the people invading our home.*

*A neighbor woman hauls buckets of water from the well and laboriously climbs the two-step wooden threshold leading into the kitchen. She grunts and stiffens her back as she lifts and pours the* buckets of water into huge pots on the stove. Wood is frequently inserted into the big black stove to keep the water boiling.

Galvanized tubs are perched on wooden sawhorses in the middle of the kitchen. Blood-stained rags are washed in one tub and rinsed in the second tub. After the rinsing, one of the women, using a slick-worn stick to prevent scalding her hands, moves the rags around in the boiling water before she gingerly pulls them out to place in cold water. She takes the cooled sterilized rags in her raw, swollen hands, wringing them tightly to be reused by the woman standing by the side of my mother's bed. Two women, struggling with the weight, carry the heavy tubs of ruby-red colored water outside through the kitchen door to dump out at the edge of the hard-packed dirt yard.

And the process continues. The filling of one tub with fresh well water and the second tub with the scalding hot water from the stove, the washing, sterilization, wringing out the rags, and the dumping of the crimson-red water. Every so often a neighbor knocks softly, peering through the screen door, and in hushed tones inquires about my mother. Neighbors bring food, offer to help and express grave concern. No one speaks to me. For once I am not the center of attention.

*Quietly I walk to the doorway of my mother's room. There is one individual who never leaves my mother's bedside. I can see beads of sweat lingering on her slightly visible mustache. Her dress sleeves are rolled high and I can see long, sparse black hair dotting her arms. I can hear her soothing voice and somehow I know this woman is keeping my mother alive. She exchanges washcloths with fresh, clean, cold ones and gently swabs my mother's face. From time to time, without turning her attention from Mother, this angel gives hurried, whispered instructions.*

*"Change the water." "Bring clean rags." "Help change the bedding." "Empty the bucket." "Help me turn Lenore." "Help me change her nightgown."*

*Mother, looking pale and small in her bed, occasionally rolls her head from side to side. Her naturally curly black hair is now straight and sticking randomly around her face. I try to keep my eyes focused on her eyes, willing her to look in my direction. I want her to see me and call me to her, but I don't think she can see me. I don't think my mother can see anyone. My mother is hemorrhaging and teetering on the brink of death.*

Mother continued to labor with the birth of her eleventh child long into the evening. Wrenched in the dregs of her physical misery, she gave birth to a baby girl who lived only a few hours. My brother Tony remembers how mother cried when Lenorcita stopped breathing. Holding the infant close to her body, Mother cooed words of endearment to deaf ears, refusing to let her go.

As soon as she was able to get out of bed after Lenorcita's death, still weak and pale, Mother harnessed her weighty belt of responsibilities and went back to work. No one argued with her to stay in bed and give her body time to heal, to get healthy and strong. No one sympathized or pitied her. We needed her services. If an opinion was voiced by anyone outside of the family about my mother's work ethics, about her poor health, about her heavy load, it was easily justified by my family. The remark-maker was assured that Mother was ambitious, headstrong, and wanted to be independent.

Mother refused to relent to weakness and never allowed herself to ask for help. I remember standing at the screen door leading out of the middle room, watching my two brothers load her treadle sewing machine onto the pickup truck. She would need it for her new job. I was crying.

*Chapter 13*

# THE BATH

Mother and I walked to Grandmother Gertrudes' house to help her work in her vegetable garden. We stopped at Lenorcita's grave along the way to leave a geranium blossom that Mother had clipped from her potted plant. Mother said a prayer, kneeling on the dirt, before we continued walking.

Grandmother, wearing a long apron and a scowl on her face, stood in the doorway as we walked up the wooden steps to her front door. It was always very stressful to be in my grandparents' home. I spent the time there worried that I would do something to upset Grandmother. Mother never cautioned me to behave. Grandmother's demeanor was sufficient.

While Mother and Grandmother worked in the garden, I got very dirty playing in the mud by the ditch. When they took a break and went into the house, Mother turned to me and quietly said, "Stay here, Rosabelle, while I warm the kitchen to give you a bath."

With my hands cupped at the sides of my face to block the light, I peered through the screen door and saw Mother put wood in the stove. She placed a tub on a wide bench in the middle of the kitchen and filled it with heated water. Back outside, Mother removed my muddy clothes and left them on the porch. She picked me up, took me into the house, and carefully placed me in the warm, soapy water. All the while Grandmother criticized my mother for letting me get dirty.

"Don't stand up, Rosabelle, or the tub will tip," Mother said in an unusually stern voice. No sooner were the words out of her mouth when, as she reached away from the tub for a towel, I stood up to reach for her. The tub tilted. Mother grabbed me in mid-air. Water gushed across the kitchen floor. A barrage of spiteful words erupted from

Grandmother's mouth as Mother wrapped me up in the towel and set me on a kitchen chair.

Poor mother! The stress around her was intense. She gathered her dress in front of her as she got down on her knees to wipe up the water. Grandmother did not offer to hold me or to help Mother. Sobbing softly, I stayed huddled, wrapped in my towel watching my mother. The confused, hurt feelings I experienced cannot compare to the crushing pain my mother must have experienced.

When Mother finished sopping up the water from the floor, she took a bucket of soapy water outside to wash my muddy clothes. Back in the house, she combed my hair and asked Grandmother for an old shirt. She slipped the large shirt over my shoulders and rolled up the sleeves, tying the front panels so they wouldn't drag. Mother winked at me, gave me a big hug, and went back to work in the garden with Grandmother. I played quietly in the house by myself, while my clothes dried on the line.

Grandpa came home. He saw me sitting on the floor and walked up to me. With a big grin on his face, he patted me on the head. "What a beautiful dress, little girl." He entered his office and closed the door. At the end of the day, wearing my clean, dry clothes, Mother and I walked home in the dark. We stumbled on the muddy and rutty road. I held my mother's hand tightly. I was hungry and tired. Mother was anxious to get home to fix dinner for us.

It's not difficult to visualize Grandmother's heavy challenges, but her sternness prevented me from ever bonding with her. I never sat on her lap. I never remember her speaking to me other than to impatiently flip her hand and shoo me out of her way.

"¡Como molestas! Quitas tu hija la de aquí."

I do remember her bent back and her long white hair, braided or rolled into a tight bun. My young mind did not make judgment, though.

# Chapter 14

# A KINDRED SPIRIT

**G**randmother Gertrudes' younger sister, Zenaida, lived in Cimarron and was near my mother's age. Zenaida was the complete opposite of her sister. She had a loving, gregarious personality, and she was a kindred spirit with my mother. I looked forward to our infrequent but endearing visits to Cimarron, which allowed us to spend time with my cheerful Great Aunt Zenaida.

Cimarron, New Mexico was a lawless haven for mountain men, trappers, gold prospectors, cowboys and outlaws. The town was built on the original Beaubien-Miranda Land Grant in 1842 before Maxwell took possession of the Grant. Roaming, rugged men visited the saloons and gambling halls, shot out lanterns and mirrors and caused many a ruckus in town. But, by the time Zenaida lived there, it had evolved into a friendlier, active community.

Mother and her aunt enjoyed their times together. Their conversations were animated and constant as they cleaned, sewed, cooked, or relaxed with a cup of coffee at the cluttered kitchen table. Their laughter brought a resounding laughter to Aunt Zenaida's son, Freddy, and me.

Once, Mother sewed a shirt for Freddy and a blouse for me, using the same print fabric. Aunt Zenaida stood back to look at us. Through pursed lips, she said, "Phew, you two are the best looking twins I have ever seen."

Freddie and I proudly looked at each other for resemblance and we happily went out to play.

By late afternoon, Mother and Zenaida stopped their housework to prepare for the community dance. While chatting happily, they speculated which of their friends would attend. Their gaiety flowed onto the children. We also waited for the time to go to the *baile*. Children were an accepted part of the dance. It was common to see the little ones dancing with one another or with one of the parents or running freely between the couples swaying to the music. Often a child could be seen sleeping on a bed made from pushing chairs together while the merriment continued late into the night.

From the very old to the very young, dancing on the dusty, wood-plank floor was a joyous occasion. My mother was graceful and popular. She glided with the waltz, slid with the Virginia reel and hopped with the polka. *Put Your Little Foot* was my favorite song. Mother taught me the steps. She loved music and also had a light delicate voice.

Great Aunt Zenaida was married to a travelling salesman, Benjamin, who was also a gambler. She loved him. He loved gambling, so was not a very good provider. Zenaida collected dirty laundry from the *Americanos*. Using her scrub board and irons heated on the stove, she made enough money to keep her family fed. Her gambling husband was gone a good deal of the time and when he was home, he was not very kind to her.

One night after a dance, Benjamin hitched a ride home for them with an acquaintance. My aunt sat between the two men and as the men talked, Mortimer, the driver, asked Benjamin to pay up on a gambling debt.

Benjamin tipped his head toward his wife. "Take her and we'll call it even."

With only a handshake, Zenaida was traded away, obligated to take her five children and live with Mortimer. It is impossible today to comprehend how little control women had over their lives.

Mortimer was good to my great-aunt and provided a secure home for her and her children. During this union they had one child. But Zenaida, I have heard, never lost her love for Benjamin. After Mortimer and my great aunt parted, she lived with a third man, Fredrico, and they had five children.

Early one morning, before the sun gave its first light, Great Aunt Zenaida got into bed between two of her young sleeping sons, Freddy and his brother. She had tied one end of a thick string to her big toe and the other end to the trigger of a .28 gauge single-shot shotgun. Aunt Zenaida held the rifle barrel snugly under her chin and stretched her toe.

A neighbor, knowing that my family had relatives in Cimarron, brought a clipping from the newspaper about a death in Cimarron to show my mother. It was my Great Aunt Zenaida. Who is to say what extent of torture a loving, passionate person can bear when held captive by her circumstances. Because she was family and not a stranger it was never talked about. Cousin Freddy never said anything to me about it and I never asked. We grieved for a high-spirited, gregarious, loving, lovable soul who left us so tragically, so unexpectedly.

*Chapter 15*

# THE OFFER

## *Ripples*

*We cause ripples
with all our actions, often
without even trying.
Good or bad some ripples result
in lifelong consequences.
Realizing the importance of
our individual ripples
one would think we would
paddle carefully
through the journey of life.*

—*ROSE SPADER*—

L ong before World War II, Grandpa M.C. had acquired land that extended from Taos eastward to the Palo Flechado Pass. He gave parcels of land east of the Taos Plaza and down the road from his house to his children on which to build their homes. Eventually the road became known as Martinez Lane.

My father built a little log cabin on my mother's lot next to Aunt Josephina's house. Memories of bundling up and walking to visit my aunts along the lane over a diamond-sprinkled blanket of snow in the winter or through fresh fields in the summer, stir me nostalgically. Their warm greetings and attention to my childish needs still make me marvel at their kindness. And, through the years, have greatly influenced my adult behavior. My Aunt Florida would let me color using her older children's coloring books, ignoring their protests. My Aunt Josefina would take time from her busy schedule to listen patiently to my childish prattle. Always, in many ways, I was given special attention from all of my tenderhearted aunts. At the end of my visits they picked vegetables from their gardens to fill a cloth sack for me to take to my mother.

My uncles would tousle my hair if I encountered them on my way home. Most of my uncles had three distinct, different personalities: drunk and verbose, hung-over and irritable, or mostly, strong, dependable, helpful, handsome and loving. They helped each other—building their homes, re-roofing, digging for a new outhouse, offering transportation—willingly giving of themselves.

Uncle Frank did not build his house on Martinez Lane. When he married Preciliana La Varta, she had already inherited a beautiful home on the outskirts of town. Aunt Pritz, as she was nicknamed, was born in 1907 in the cold San Juan Basin of southern Colorado, the second of seven children. When she was three, her mother, expecting her third baby, decided Pritz would stay with her grandmother in Taos. As time passed more children were born, and a time for Pritz to move back home to her family was never convenient. Pritz was raised as an only child by a loving grandmother. During that time, it was not uncommon for relatives to help a burdened family by raising one of the children.

Aunt Pritz told me that her grandmother, an industrious head of the household, rented rooms in her large home on Pueblo Road. Tenants were mostly aspiring artists or newcomers relocating to our little village. Most of these visitors came from the eastern part of the United States and spoke little, if any, Spanish. To my charismatic, spirited aunt, this communication barrier needed to be corrected.

My aunt told me there was an old wooden bench painted a bright aqua-blue, which sat as a sentry of welcome inside the adobe-wall-enclosed patio near the entrance of her grandmother's home.

"Rosabelle," Aunt Pritz said, "When I was only about six, I would sit on that bench and smile. As visitors passed the bench to inquire about renting a room or heading to a rented room, they would see me and ask, *"How are you, little girl?"* I would repeat their words, "How are you, little girl?" with my hands clasped in my lap and my legs swinging."

Time and time again, whatever English conversation may have been directed toward Aunt Pritz, she responded by repeating what she heard. That's how she learned and spoke her new language without an accent.

After Pritz married into Mother's family, she and Mother developed a special bond. These two women were not matriarchs, they were humanitarians. They were motivated by compassion, not hampered by jealousy, envy, or competition. Their selflessness brought them closer to each other. Both women believed in giving without the expectation of receiving.

I can still hear their words of wisdom. Mother would say, "Be especially kind to orphans. There is no greater loss than the loss of a parent's love!" Or she would remark, "Loneliness is the worst sickness in the world."

Aunt Pritz used to tell us to kiss a newborn baby. "Honey, babies are pure, spotless, and full of the Holy Spirit. They came here straight from God."

I stay inspired by women with such benevolence.

These women, as did most women of my mother's era, had little control over their lives. A husband's word was law. A woman would not question his actions, including harsh punishment of their children. If a divorce occurred, it was most likely the husband who initiated the action. A divorced woman would frequently be ostracized and suffer retribution from her family and friends.

We were Catholics in a community that considered large families a blessing from God. It was His providence, and any intervention was not condoned. A husband had the right to be disrespectful if his wife tended toward easy conceptions and they already had a large family. Or if he wanted a son and only daughters were born.

Women did not deny their husband's needs. If a couple did not conceive, the woman was blamed with the assumption that all men were potent.

In the same year as Lenorcita's death, one of Mother's younger sisters, Gregoria, gave birth to a baby girl. Uncle Frank, Mother, and I were among the many relatives visiting the family to offer blessings and good wishes to the new baby. Merriment filled my aunt's house. Amid laughter and loud discussions, children of various ages played and fought, running freely in and out of her blessed home. Children came in to eat, complain or cry about a slight wound. They were fed or comforted and then sent back out to play.

Clustered in typical male camaraderie out in the yard, the men joked and teased as they shared swigs from a bottle. At times, they directed their teasing to the younger boys, tripping them and laughing at them when they fell. Though sometimes harsh and offensive, it was a form of communication, a token of recognition. If a mother or aunt happened to intervene, it would result in the child's further humiliation, "What are you, a baby—hiding behind a woman's skirt—can't you take it? I was just kidding."

Inside, frijoles, tortillas, papitas, chile, and chicharrones were continuously prepared and generously served. Aunt Gregoria, burping her newborn, gently talked to her two-year-old son who was suffering from sibling rivalry. It was in this clamor of family unity that Uncle Frank took the baby from his sister's arms. Cuddling the infant close to his chest, he unabashedly and quite passionately asked her to let him keep the baby. He emotionally pointed out to his sister that she already had her hands full with a large family.

While pacing back and forth in front of my aunt, who was now holding her neglected two-year-old, Uncle Frank emphasized the fact that she could have more children. He made reference to his secure financial situation. Didn't his sister understand that butchers made good money, that neither he nor Pritz would ever be without work? With a bold masculine superiority, he assured his sister that he was in a far better position to raise the child.

Except for Uncle Frank, all of Grandmother's children were blessed with large families. He was desperate to be a parent. Tears filled his eyes as he gently readjusted the baby's blanket. But, arrogant and confident, Uncle Frank also felt justified in asking for the baby, never considering that the proposition would be offensive to his sister.

Gregoria apologetically declined her brother's request. My mother felt compassion for her younger brother. Having just lost Baby Lenorcita and believing that her childbearing days were likely behind her, Mother tried to placate her brother. On a whim, she told him that she would have a hazel-eyed, fair-skinned baby boy who looked just like him. It would be a child that would make him proud and bring him happiness—a child to call his own. *"Un niño, solo para ti, Hermano,"* she told him.

As far back as I can remember, I have had a gnawing awareness that there was an unspoken desire to have fair-skinned children in our community. I never wanted to be any other shade than the shade I am, but my sister Carolyn and my brother Tony took great pride in their light skin, believing it confirmed their heritage from Spain. The Hispanic population at the time was overly concerned about proving their European lineage, and it was impossible not to notice the bias.

All children were loved, but a more tolerant and praising attitude was expressed when communicating with lighter-skinned children. The Catholic nuns frequently selected a *huerra* as teacher's pet. Light eyes or blond hair were an added bonus, but light skin alone was sufficient to merit special consideration.

My brother Ernest had dark skin and was measured by a different yardstick. His intelligence, good looks, and amiable, highly spirited personality did not spare him from the bias: *pobrecito, es curiosito pero tan negrito.* Despite this bias, Ernest was always the most popular of my parents' children. Be that as it may, my uncle took my mother's offer to heart. Uncle Frank returned the little infant to his sister. Her two-year-old, now reinforced by his mother's love, went out to play and let the screen door slam in his wake.

At many of our family gatherings, I remember my Uncle Frank identifying strongly with a nephew or niece, bribing the child to go live with him and Aunt Pritz. He was not biased making his selection. He just wanted a child to call his own. Uncle Frank would pull a handful of coins from his pocket and, with exaggerated fanfare, offer it to the child. If that didn't work, he would promise other tangible things: a BB-gun, a leather jacket, a trip to town, candy, or holding the steering wheel in his truck. At times the bribe would be timidly accepted—accepted, that is, until it was time to leave the party. Like my cousins, I remember being tempted when my uncle would approach me. But now, with the offer, Uncle Frank, so desperate to have a child, could breathe easy and be happy in anticipation. His sister, my mother, would soon have a fair-skinned, hazel-eyed son for him to call his own.

# Chapter 16

# THE PROMISE

A few months after that happy gathering at Aunt Gregoria's house, my mother became pregnant with her twelfth child. Of her eleven previous pregnancies, six had resulted in death. Jose Emilio, named after my dad's deceased father, died before his second birthday. Then Beatrice and Carolyn were born. Next, Ildefonso, named after my dad, was born unhealthy and lived only about eight months. Ernest and Tony were born, then a miscarriage. Eulalia Priscilla lived only about six months. Valentino, born on Valentine's Day, was her ninth child, but lived only about one month.

After Valentino, I was born. Finally baby Lenorcita was born. And now, this pregnancy came as she was nearing menopause.

I know little of how my brothers and sisters died. Mother did not talk about it and I never asked.

With Mother's new pregnancy, a pregnancy she thought could not happen and with the weight of her promise to her brother, Mother did not look to her alcoholic husband for help. Neither did she rely on her children. Mother did not even consider asking support from *her* mother. She certainly didn't need her mother's harassment. She knew, without question, that Grandmother Gertrudes would take her son Frank's position and insist the promise be kept.

Defeated, tormented, and pressured to hold true to her promise, Mother must have made an extraordinarily difficult choice to hide her pain and move forward. Mother did not need another mouth to feed and worry about. The lightly given promise that she feared her brother had taken seriously loomed heavy in her heart. In an unrealistic effort to keep the pregnancy a secret and fearing the loss of her child, she decided to move the family to Santa Fe from the split-log cabin my dad had built on her tract of land.

Immediately after we arrived in Santa Fe, the capital of New Mexico, Mother found a house for us off the main road on Rosario Street. It was ten blocks from where she found a job with the White Swan Laundry. Forty-two-years-old and pregnant, she stood on swollen feet for long hours pushing a heavy, hot iron that had been heated on a coal-burning stove.

There was no coming home at the end of a long workday to put her feet up and rest. No prenatal care or necessary vitamins. No indulging unusual cravings. After her workday at the laundry, Mother returned home to cook, sew, clean house, and give us love and acceptance. Mother was always active and at times impatient, sometimes restless, but never helpless. She never implied that her load was too heavy. If ever she was caught with a tear in her eye she made light of it.

"Nothing is wrong, I have something in my eye," she would say.

It was while living in our house in Santa Fe that my brother Tony found a roll of copper wire from which he made rings by twisting the wire into interesting designs. Hunched over a wooden box using pliers to twist the wire he'd say, "I'm going to be rich selling these rings, Rosabelle."

I believed him and we made plans for what he would buy with all his money. I am quite sure my brother's dream was influenced by my mother's desire to improve our destiny—a desire she instilled in all of us, if not by words, by her actions.

When Dad was sober, he did contract labor work such as forming the foundation for a new house or digging a water trench. He would wake my brothers up early in the morning and after breakfast, with Mother's prepared lunch in hand, head for the job site. They worked all day and came home for supper and returned to work till dark. Both boys worked, but when Tony got tired Dad let him sit down for a short time while praising his work. If Ernest wanted to rest, Dad berated him and pushed him to work harder. Jamming the shovel into the dirt in front of Ernest, he would harshly say, "Act like a man." Though Dad was strict with my brothers and sisters, neither Dad nor Mother were strict raising me.

Dad and my brothers would scout along the railroad tracks for pieces of coal dropped from the steam-operated trains to use for fuel in our house. One time Dad found an old, large church bell half buried in a dried-up arroyo. I can only assume that this bell once hung in a church tower built by the Spanish Catholic missionaries.

The story is told that he hauled this bell into town in the little wooden pull-wagon they used to transport the coal. In town he discussed the bell with a friend who advised him to talk to an attorney. He did. And the attorney bought the bell for fifty dollars, promising Dad the bell would be exhibited in a museum. Dad was happy with the much-needed money and did not ask where the bell would be housed. He did not consider the historical implications of such a valuable find. To this day, the whereabouts of the bell is unknown to my family.

During this time in Santa Fe, while waiting for the new baby, my brothers, twelve and fourteen years old, enrolled in their new school. But their attendance was secondary to Dad's contract work. My brothers also found odd jobs on weekends. Ernest hawked the newspaper from a corner newsstand.

At other times, my brother delivered papers door-to-door on his pieced-together bicycle. Some mornings, as Ernest pedaled, Tony sat on the handlebars, tossing the rolled-up newspapers. Carolyn enrolled in the tenth grade and after school helped an old spinster, Miss Delia Harris, with odd jobs. By then, Bea lived on her own. Everyone, except my dad who had infrequent jobs and me, was busy helping to keep bread on the table.

Occasionally, Dad found work such as sweeping out a grocery store. When it was necessary for the store to throw out non-sellable food, Dad retrieved it. Mother would clean it and cook the usable parts. Most of the time, however, Dad drank. Money was scarce, and our family was having a difficult time. The year was 1938, toward the end of the Great Depression and before World War II.

As fall turned to winter, Mother's pregnancy became more difficult. I sat at the kitchen table and watched her slice potatoes and crack fresh eggs into a hot cast-iron skillet. I could hear the sizzling. The aroma made me hungry. With her hand supporting her back, alleviating the weight of the unborn child within her, Mother served our breakfast. A pot of beans for our lunch simmered on the wood-burning stove. On the counter, Mother set out fresh tortillas wrapped in a towel.

"The beans will be ready by lunch," she said, inserting a piece of kindling into the stove. Turning toward my brother, she said, "Tony, be sure to keep the fire burning."

She picked up her purse and gloves from the bench and told me, "Be good, Rosabelle." Placing her hand lovingly under my chin to lift my face, she kissed my forehead and walked out the door.

Not long after she arrived at the White Swan Laundry and started ironing, her water broke. In the throes of labor, Mother hurried home to give birth to a baby she was determined to keep.

Mother arranged with a midwife to help her through the delivery. Together, those two brave women brought forth a beautiful, fair-skinned baby boy, Leonard Edgar Manuel Sandoval. Mother added the name Edgar in honor of the kind midwife's son.

The news of the blessed event was soon carried to Taos, or maybe my Uncle Frank knew of my mother's pregnancy from the onset. Either way, shortly after my little brother's birth, my mother opened the door to see her brother standing there, teeming with confidence and full of happy expectations.

But my uncle and aunt's visit was not as agreeable or rewarding as they had expected. Instead of a bouncing baby boy they found my uncle's dream-come-true baby very much in need of medical attention. The baby was shockingly undernourished, sick and very weak, lying in a little box at the foot of the bed.

They found my mother drawn and haggard, wearing a strained, newly-gaunt look. She, too, was undernourished and weakened by her pregnancy, the recent birth, and the family's grievous financial circumstances. Her dedicated mothering efforts came short of meeting the demands of her family's depressed circumstances and were insufficient to alter the baby's dire condition.

The baby's frailty was fuel for Uncle Frank. Speaking in a firm tone, he reminded my mother, "You made a promise!"

My mother turned her back to my uncle to hide her tears.

"This baby needs to go to a doctor, Lenore," he demanded. "Give me the baby before he dies!"

Mother knew the baby's condition was grave. She did not doubt my uncle's sincerity or ability, but still she refused. Failing with his first approach, Uncle Frank begged Mother to come with the baby to his home in Taos so he could, at least, provide medical care for my little brother.

Mother was torn between leaving her family and facing the possibility of losing her newborn son. The kind midwife who had helped my mother through the birth predicted the baby would only live a short time. In a lame effort to forestall her brother's demand, Mother told him she did not want to give him a child who was going to die. Ultimately, Uncle Frank and Aunt Pritz returned to Taos without his promised child.

Shortly after Uncle Frank and Aunt Pritz visited with us in Santa Fe, Grandpa M.C. came to visit. He brought a truckload of much-needed firewood. He and my mother were very close, and his concern for her prompted his visit.

Trying not to show how shocked he was with her situation, Grandpa sympathized with his daughter. "What can I do to help you, Lenore?" he asked, reaching across the table to hold her hands. "I will help you any way I can."

Mother's face crumbled as she looked at her father. "I don't know what to do."

They talked, analyzing her options. She reluctantly accepted the harsh fact that without Frank's help she could not provide adequate care for the baby. By the end of her father's visit, Mother asked him to take the baby and her with him on his return trip to Taos. She hoped that with medical intervention the baby would live. But she refused to entertain the thought that by going to Taos, she might have to fulfill her promise. She refused to worry about how her family would weather her absence. Because I was too little to be left alone, I was taken to Taos along with the baby.

We bounced along the winding canyon road in Grandpa's large and noisy, lumber truck. Mother held the baby. I sat in the middle between Grandpa and Mother. After a long ride, we arrived at Uncle Frank and Aunt Pritz's large adobe home.

Manicured, short-cropped grass covered the ground all the way from the porch to a small river where I could see ducks pleasantly preening their feathers. Sheep were feeding in the nearby field. Lush meadows, spotted with early blooming wild purple irises, filled the air with fragrance. Hearing the noisy lumber truck approach, my aunt and uncle, and Great Aunt Cacaya trailing behind, rushed out of the house to greet us. They helped carry our few belongings onto their long front porch. They couldn't do enough to make us comfortable.

Mother and Aunt Pritz embraced. Aunt Pritz may not have agreed with her husband about the promise, but she could not say so, even in private. The compassion between these two women would see them through another family crisis. Cacaya held my hand as we walked into the house. I felt very important and it made me happy that my mother was so loved.

Special accommodations had been made for the baby. All the furniture had been cleared from a room and replaced with a crib and rocking chair. Even the window curtains had been changed. Aunt

Pritz told Mother preparations for the baby had all been done before their visit to Santa Fe.

We were in Taos only a short time before the doctor arrived. From that very moment, Baby Leonard had constant attention. My little brother was made comfortable without consideration of cost or effort. The doctor visited the nursery daily, and his orders were carried out to the letter. Mother and Aunt Pritz hardly slept, keeping a constant vigil over the baby's crib. Uncle Frank stayed home from work and spent much of his time sitting in the baby's room hunched over with his elbows resting on his knees, his head cradled in his hands, quietly waiting for movement from the little crib. Sadly, no amount of care or attention improved my little brother's health, and he continued to hover between life and death.

I was only about four years old, but I clearly remember my mother's heavy heart. I remember Aunt Pritz and Cacaya staying close by her, watching and silently waiting, praying for the baby to get better, fearful the baby might die, and waiting for Mother to make a decision. With hushed whispers, these kind, gentle-hearted women comforted my mother.

Aunt Pritz always kept a spotless house and tirelessly waited on my uncle. He, in turn, made disparaging remarks about her efforts, grunted unintelligible answers to her questions, and gave her disapproving looks whenever their eyes met.

She never showed anger, rejection, or pain, just silent resolve. Her communication to him was always at his convenience. If his mood was dark, she waited to ask her question. When he cut her down too sharply, she remained silent. And it would be in this pristine but dictatorial and submissive environment that my baby brother was destined to live. A memory of a scene in the kitchen stands out in my mind like a photograph held in my hand.

*I see my mother and Aunt Pritz near the window by the caged canaries. Cacaya is sitting on a short, three-legged wooden stool beside a potbelly stove in the corner of the large kitchen. After pulling a cloth bag of tobacco and folder of cigarette-making paper from her apron pocket, Cacaya slowly rolls and licks the edge of the paper with her tongue to seal the cigarette. She strikes a large kitchen match on the potbelly stove, and lights the cigarette, holding it between her thumb and index finger. Periodically she wipes her face with the corner of her long apron.*

*Uncle Frank, looking very somber, startles me as he abruptly enters the kitchen. The three women are silent and stressed. In a stern voice, my uncle tells my mother that God will take the baby if she does not keep her promise. His face turns red as he yells, "You must want the baby to die, Lenore!" He tells her she should not have made the promise if she had not intended to keep her word. I think my uncle is drinking. Mother wipes tears from her face, but she does not look up as Uncle Frank, full of rage, leaves the kitchen.*

The burden of this decision was beyond comprehension. To resolve the dilemma, Uncle Frank would have to acknowledge his sister's pain and let go of his dream to have a child, and that he could not do. Mother was plagued with guilt. Either option burdened her heart. *What if she declined and the baby died? How could she give her child away?* Having already endured the pain of losing six children did not lessen my mother's anguish. Only her strength of character and the hope that a doctor's care might save her baby made it possible to live through this painful episode.

Like the Bible story, in which two harlots claim to be the mother of the same child. King Solomon ordered the baby cut in half, knowing that the real mother would rather disclaim her parentage than have the baby killed. Thus, he was able to determine which one of the two women was the baby's mother. King Solomon was a wise man and he had a difficult judgment to make, but his method of proving parentage clearly shows that it was not *his* baby.

After long sleepless nights and tormented days, with no sign of the baby's health improving, Mother finalized her decision to give her baby to my aunt and uncle. Maybe the result of her decision is exaggerated, but miraculously, the baby's health showed an immediate improvement. Uncle Frank was beside himself with joy. He lifted Baby Leonard from the crib, cooing to him, and cradled him close to his chest. My blessed Mother resolved to make the situation amicable.

The need to stay in Taos was negated by the finality of Mother's decision. Quietly resigned, Mother and I returned to Santa Fe. Mother did not indulge herself with pity. She needed to be home to take care of her family and to crowd her days with activity, and thus, ward off the crushing feelings of loneliness and loss. She could not allow herself to feel hopeless. She could only keep moving or depression would overtake her. She needed to be strong.

Yes, Mother and I left this pristine environment—this lovely home with varnished wood floors and the only indoor toilet I had ever used, this house that had a pleasant smell with furnishings that gleamed dust free as the sunshine filtered through spotlessly clean windows. We left this house with the bright yellow caged canaries chirping over the kitchen bay window. Mother and I left the love of two doting aunts and an abundance of food. We left the little child's chair that had been set out just for me. We left the peaceful sound of the river water where I watched ducks sunning themselves and listened to bleating sheep.

We returned to Santa Fe, leaving my baby brother, my mother's last-born child, now sporting a new surname, Leonard Edgar Manuel *Martinez*. I will never in my lifetime be able to comprehend the pain my mother endured. She made no attempt to justify her decision. She quietly and independently carried the burden.

It goes without saying, that our need to be in Santa Fe also ended. A short time after our return to Santa Fe from this traumatic trip, my family moved back to Taos. I have no real memory of my dad, sisters or brothers sympathizing with my mother over the loss of Baby Leonard. Even as the years passed, I do not remember Leonard's parentage as a focus of attention or conversation. He always knew that his real parents were J.I. and Lenore but he never asked why he lived with Aunt Pritz and Uncle Frank.

*Chapter 17*

# PERIODS OF SOBRIETY

S ome people live life with a sense of balance. They are not derailed by poor health, a bad marriage, excessive poverty, continually squashed goals, or, God forbid, the loss of a child. These people are too busy fulfilling their obligations to take time off for self-pity. These people prioritize their giving before their taking. My mother was such a person.

I remember a deep sadness in my mother. Most assuredly she was suffering from the loss of her last two children, Lenorcita and Leonard. When criticized by her relatives for letting her brother keep Leonard, she knew she would have been judged just as harshly if she had kept her child, who had been failing to thrive in their impoverished condition. My mother's family was also critical of my father for his lack of concern for his family's needs, for his drinking, and for his neglectful treatment of my mother. But they voiced their opinions only to Mother.

Years later, with blatant disregard for my feelings and insensitivity to my mother's pain, Carolyn quoted one of Dad's past comments to me. "Rosabelle, you don't have anyone to play with. Your mother gave your little companion away."

Dad was never held accountable for his drinking. How did Mother not retaliate, yell that they could not care for the baby because her husband drank and did not provide for his family? How did she not voice her pain or her anger at him? Where was my dad when my mother needed support? Why didn't he assert himself to intervene and ask Uncle Frank for help in caring for the baby so Mother could keep her child?

From the time he was very young, Dad had worked in many occupations from foreman to blacksmith, carpenter to butcher, horseman to farmer. With his loyal dog by his side, Dad freighted food supplies to Peñasco, his horses pulling the load. Dad was unassuming and non-judgmental. He was also a good, albeit, stern father and a nonintrusive husband who allowed my mother latitude that most men of that day would not have condoned.

My brothers and sisters tell me our dad was a remarkable and respected man. Hardworking, kind-hearted, and strikingly good-looking, some said he had a John Wayne persona. But at times, Dad made decisions without considering the long-term effect on his family. He had a fast, flash temper. And when he felt unjustly treated, he retaliated by getting into a fistfight or quitting his job. Dad was a drinker who embraced his bottle before his family. My brothers and sisters tell me when they were young, my dad slept with a bottle and a gun under his pillow.

By the time we moved to Santa Fe, by the time I knew him, the years and the drinking had taken a toll on him. He had been reduced to a wino and a binge drinker who, on occasion, stole from his family to satisfy his habit. I was saddened to learn that when we lived in Santa Fe, waiting for Baby Leonard to be born and having such a difficult time, Dad had exchanged a new pair of Sunday shoes given to me by a relative for a bottle at the local watering hole.

Employers were eager to hire him in times of sobriety, but when his drinking bouts took him, he was a non-person, unkempt, staggering and blabbering foolishness, even when no one was listening. When he was too weak to buy a bottle, he drank anything containing alcohol from our kitchen and bathroom cabinets. While employed by a grocery store in Taos, Dad even drank the vanilla from the basement supply area.

Gradually, Dad's drinking periods lasted longer, and his body recovered more slowly. After a number of months, sometimes a couple of years of sobriety, Dad would start drinking again. During the sober periods, my parents made steps to improve our lot. But once on the bottle, Dad did not stop drinking until the liquor had saturated his body and depleted his health and logic. Alcohol transformed a healthy, good man into a physically wasted, helpless, pitiful, repentant, skinny, and sick weakling. After each drinking bout, Dad became less involved in his family responsibilities and Mother became more restless and more determined to alter our situation.

Disappointed, disillusioned, hurt, and full of repugnance, she would, nonetheless, nurse him back to health. Mother would remove and throw away his long-worn, stinky clothes, bathe his wasted body, and support his shaking hands as he drank warmed blue corn *atole* or gulped raw eggs she broke into a cup. She helped him until the varmints in his delirious mind stopped crawling on the walls, stopped attacking his body, not giving up until the blackouts and withdrawal symptoms stopped. She helped him until the color came back to his skin and logic came back to his brain. She helped him gain weight and become a good man again. As time passed, she became more and more determined and believed less and less his promise never to drink again.

But drunk or sober, Dad was treated in our home with the paternal respect instilled in children. Dad's drinking created a psychological and financial teeter-totter—harsh, disruptive periods for my mother and family. Adjusting from a sober Dad to a drinking Dad, or the opposite, was always difficult. We were happy when he stopped drinking, but our ways had to change to accommodate a nice, contented man.

Mother never accepted his drinking as involuntary. However, she never let it diminish her sense of responsibility to her children, to her husband, or to life in general. We never acknowledged to Mother that it was her perseverance that supported us through the tough times—financially and emotionally. Instead, we blamed *her* for Dad's drinking.

Mother juggled her life to meet our needs. She refused to waste time on regrets or self-pity, and did not tolerate those who did. Never a sycophant, she understood personalities and told it how it was. Mother rejected complacency and she did not accept excuses. She was not impressed with status or wealth, nor appalled by poverty. Rich or poor, clean or dirty, young or old, Mother was in her element with humanity. Mother loved children and was kind to animals.

Mother was an interesting storyteller, and she used her stories as anecdotes when others were troubled. She was never idle, never too busy for a friend in need. Even while rolling out a tortilla or cutting fabric, she would disagree or compliment, rejoice with her visitors or give advice. "To distract myself from troubling thoughts, I get down on my hands and knees and scrub the floors." She would say. "Marry the man you love, a life without love is a very lonely life."

When some friends left, others came. Mother would get up from her sewing machine to replenish the food or make a fresh pot of coffee. Her fortitude was visible, unusual, and silent as she worked tirelessly to lift the spirits of neighbors, friends, or relatives and to distract her mind and heart from her losses.

On the day Grandpa M.C. died, Dad held my mother close in his arms and they cried together. My brother Ernest carried me. My dad held my mother's hand as my family walked the path to Tio Luciano and Tia Florida's home. The stories of why Grandpa M.C. was living with them and not with Grandmother Gertrudes differ. Perhaps it was more peaceful, or perhaps Grandmother had kicked him out. It is rumored Grandmother Gertrudes accused Grandpa of supporting another man's wife. She could have been referring to one of her married daughters. Or not.

Still, Grandmother Gertrudes held Grandpa's wake in the fastidiously clean room reserved for her social activities. It is the only time I remember being in that room. As if there were not enough people mourning his death, Grandmother Gertrudes hired mourners, as was customary in those days, to cry and howl over his casket, feigning grief to honor the deceased.

The night after Grandpa M.C. was laid to rest, Mother was silent. She went to her room, closed her door, and cried. The next day she resumed her responsibilities, but it was months before she was her naturally happy self again. Throughout her life,

Mother's eyes welled with tears whenever she talked about her father. With her hands clasped to her heart, she would say, "I still think of him every day and wish he were here."

# PART II

**Rosabelle standing by the fruit cellar
her father built seventy-five years ago.**

*Chapter 18*

# OASIS

As adults, we forget that children, even at the age of four or five, have a keen understanding of their circumstances and they need to be involved. Less than a year after Leonard's birth, we moved from Taos to Corrales. No one talked to me about this monumental move that would take me away from familiar people and surroundings. I created my own understanding, joyous anticipation mingled with confusion, which raced through my blood as I watched the preparation for our departure. I remember the emotional havoc I felt as

I watched the house in Taos change from a warm, happy home to a vacant space.

Pillowcases and sheets protected the breakable items. Larger pieces were wrapped with quilts. The last of our belongings were piled near the door ready to load. The place where I had been happy and excited and sad and worried now vibrated with the activity of moving. It left me unsure where *I* would fit with the changes happening in our lives.

The arrival of Uncle Alex, one of Mother's younger brothers, confirmed the reality of our departure. Friends and neighbors helped load all our worldly belongings onto Uncle Alex's flatbed truck. The truck bed had tall fence-like wobbly boards that were used to secure the larger pieces of furniture. Mother's sewing machine, our main source of income, was handled with care. Dishes, clothes, bedding, and pictures were packed in boxes, gunnysacks, wooden crates, and buckets.

Because the truck's wobbly wood-railings threatened to pull apart, every possession was carefully evaluated. Many were given away to relatives or neighbors. My uncle threw ropes crisscross over the top of the stacked items and secured the ropes to the truck. Skippy, my dear cat was the last to be loaded. She was put into a gunnysack that was securely tied with a wire to prevent her escape. The sack was then placed in an empty box in a protected area in one corner of the huge truck bed.

I cried and worried about my kitty's confusion. "Please let me hold her on my lap," I begged.

Mother's answer was a definite, "No, Rosabelle!" as she continued sweeping the last remnants of dust in the empty house.

When the loading was complete and the empty, clean house inspected, I hugged my best friend Lisha Avila goodbye. We both cried. Mother let me wear the store-bought dress with an attached vest Lisha had given me as a parting gift. Our mothers were not only neighbors, they were long-time good friends, and they took time to share a sad goodbye. Our neighbors and friends gathered around us to wish us good luck. With God's blessing, and with hugs and tears behind us, we climbed up into the cab of the truck. Looking back through the cracked window, Mother and I waved as the truck left the yard. We headed south, leaving behind the little house with morning glories climbing on the wire fences, and my birthplace. For me, Santa Fe had been far, far from Taos. For me, Corrales was on the moon.

The truck had a strong, rank odor from the combination of old age, burnt oil, and settled dust. I sat on a torn leather seat between Uncle Alex and Mother, keeping my legs clear of the long gearshift topped with a big black ball. My uncle's hand rested on that ball and, at times, he would move the gearshift, producing a grinding sound and a jerking motion. With my eyes level to the top of the dashboard, I quietly entertained myself watching the treetops and power line poles fly by. I challenged my body to keep in place whenever we hit a rut in the road or my uncle came to a sudden stop. All in all, for me, it was a long, uneventful, boring trip.

My uncle's disparaging comments on that trip still ring in my ears. He disapproved of Mother leaving her hometown and family to meet my dad in Corrales. He found Mother too independent by "trying to fill the shoes of a man." Uncle Alex counseled her to stop trying to be better than God intended her to be. "Stop putting on airs, Lenore." He rolled his eyes, asserting that even God could not understand why she would go back to her drinking husband. "You should be happy with what you have and stop being so impatient."

My mother did not attempt to justify her decision or counter my uncle's criticism. She held fast to her vision of the opportunities to be had by moving. She listened silently as the wheels on the truck, as well as in her brain, rolled onward. Mother knew her brother was voicing, albeit harshly, his concern for her.

During this trip to Corrales, I remember whispering to my mother that I was thirsty and needed to use the bathroom. The Mason glass jar filled with water was empty. My uncle, grumbling that we were losing time, slid the truck to a stop at the edge of the road near the embankment of the Rio Grande. The grade down to the river was steep. I remember my mother and me sliding and slipping over large rocks and loose ground before we got to the water's edge. After helping me "take care of my business," Mother held on to a dead tree stump and stretched out until she was able to reach the rushing water. She filled a tin cup to satisfy my thirst. She then refilled the water jar. While struggling to get up the steep grade from the river to the road Mother lost her footing and slipped, gashing her knee on a rock. Without a cry of pain, she quickly inspected her wound and the tear on her stocking. Then we continued up the riverbank. She did not mention her hurt knee to my uncle or make me feel it was my fault. I remember she apologized to my uncle for the delay. Without acknowledging her apology, my uncle turned the key. With gears grinding and a couple of jerks, we were again on our way south.

We left the poorly paved main route to Albuquerque to travel on a dusty, rutty road to get to the peaceful riverside village of Corrales. In 1939, the small, quiet, farming community was recognized for its wineries and orchards. The race to move back to the country had not yet begun. Small adobe homes were spaced amid vast farming acreages. Pruned orchards were full of blossoms, and neat, straight-furrowed rows of climbing grapevines rushed by as our truck left its dust trail.

We passed a horse-pulled hay wagon with its load stacked high above its wooden rails. The wagon driver nodded, tipping his cap. I saw two farmers breaking from their work to visit as they met where their freshly hoed fields adjoined. Their horses stayed tethered to their plows, shifting their weight, tails swishing back and forth to discourage the flies. Another farmer stumbled over dirt clods behind a handheld plow as his horse strained to pull through hardened, sun baked earth. Along the ditch were men wearing denim bib overalls, lifting channel locks to release water to irrigate their crops. In the yards, clotheslines sagging full of fresh wash swayed in the breeze. Hoists to slaughter pigs or cows were set up away from the houses.

I had never seen so much in so short a time. My family in Taos planted vegetables in little plots behind their houses. Here the farm settings seemed endless, allowing me to daydream about running through the fields. Everyone waved a greeting and turned to stare at the overloaded truck.

To me, and especially to my mother, Corrales was an oasis. Just what my mother was looking for—away from painful memories, away from judgmental relatives, away from the limitations placed upon us by circumstance. And best, away from Dad's drinking buddies. It was a fresh, new start. I can still hear Mother saying, "Now we're getting somewhere."

After about six hours, the old truck stopped in front of a large, thick-walled adobe house with a picket fence around the front yard. Dad came running out of the house, letting the kitchen screen door slam behind him. Unable to lift the gate latch fast enough, he lifted his foot, and with one swift kick he whacked the gate down. Practically all at the same time, he hugged my mother, he hugged me, and he shook hands with Uncle Alex. I was happy to finally be out of the big, stinky, wobbly, bouncing old truck, but my dad was happy to see his wife.

The first item unloaded from the truck was my cat. Released from the gunnysack, Skippy was very confused, but she showed her appreciation by purring and nudging my face with her nose. She was placed in the house for fear she would run away. Meanwhile, Dad and Uncle Alex continued to unload our belongings so my uncle could get back to Taos.

Fifteen years later, Uncle Alex lost his life in a trucking accident. He was hauling a load of logs through the canyon just outside of Taos when a snowstorm moved in. On an icy hairpin turn, Uncle Alex lost control of the heavily loaded truck, slid off the road, and plunged to the bottom of the ravine. Logs broke loose from their bindings, trapping my uncle in the truck. A search was initiated but the truck could not be seen from the road. It was days before the over-turned truck caught the attention of a man travelling slowly on a horse-drawn wagon.

By the time help arrived, my poor Uncle Alex was no longer alive. Recovering his body, evidence of his struggle to free himself from the rubble was heartbreaking. His bloodied, frozen fingers had been worn to the bone and the heels of his shoes were gone, exposing his bloody feet. My Tia Minnie was left to mourn the loss with her seven young children. Everyone mourned the loss of a husband, father, brother, son, and friend.

Located on the bend of the road that led to the Catholic Church and across the dirt road from the cemetery, our new home was a beautiful, large five-room adobe house. The thick walls allowed for deep window seats—ample space for me to sit in the sunshine and hold Skippy or for Mother's potted geraniums. A fine apple orchard, a couple of Bing cherry trees, established grape vines, and a big quince tree left plenty of room for my dad to plant green chile, corn, watermelons, cantaloupe, and tomatoes. He quartered potatoes and planted them in mounds away from the other vegetables. Paradise, right here on earth!

Some say the money from the old bell Dad found in Santa Fe was used as a down payment on the house in Corrales. But at the time, we were in too much need of money to consider saving for the future. Maybe Mother was able to save enough for the down payment, or maybe Dad had a job and paid with his monthly paycheck. I don't know the source of this bonanza, but I do know that fifty dollars was the down payment on this large adobe house that sat on the edge of a three-acre lot, adjacent to a full-running ditch. And for this house and prime parcel of land on Old Church Road, the total price was $900.

From this lovely adobe house in Corrales we could see the wire fence that surrounded the cemetery. Small picket fences surrounded the more cared-for graves. Some graves were adorned with handmade wooden crosses, which in turn were adorned with sun-faded artificial flowers. There were a few prominent marble headstones shouting the importance the occupant had held on this earth. The ground was loose sand and weeds struggled to grow on the lonely, unkempt graves. I was terrified of the place. On our way to visit our good neighbors, the Griego family, we would pass the cemetery. Holding on to my mother's hand, I imagined tugging at my heels. I knew the dead were trying to pull me into their catacomb.

Behind our home and across the dirt road from the cemetery was the old San Ysidro Catholic Church. While attending mass, we sat on benches and knelt on the wooden floor. In the corner on the right side of the altar hung a large handcrafted wood *bulto* of Christ nailed to the cross, replete with a painted black beard and a thorny crown. Painted blood dripping from his wounds, he sorrowfully looked down upon us.

Nestled in a little nook to the left of the altar was a replica of the Blessed Virgin Mary. Dressed in a light blue gown, she wore a white lace veil and looked lovingly at the Baby Jesus she held in her arms. The altar was covered with layers of heavily starched embroidered linens. Every other Sunday, a priest visited our little village to say mass and offer Holy Communion. As the parishioners entered the little church, the bare wood floor creaked and groaned. All heads turned to see who was attending, but not my mother's. She would not allow me to look back, either.

We were not as poor in Corrales as we had been in Santa Fe. With her childbearing days truly behind her, and with the warmer climate, friendly neighbors, and exciting new challenges, my mother's health improved. Life settled down and appeared less hectic.

For the most part, my brothers and sisters were no longer living at home. We rarely saw my sister Bea. She was a beauty operator and lived in Albuquerque. Carolyn was working at Creamland Dairy and spent weekends with us. My brothers, Ernest and Tony, were working in Albuquerque too, but came to visit us frequently. For a time both my brothers worked with the Civilian Conservation Corps.

The CCC was a project initiated by President Franklin D. Roosevelt to boost the morale of unemployed people after World War II. One of the biggest tasks was soil conservation. Millions of trees were planted to restore areas eroded by heavy lumbering and wildfires.

On many cold mornings, Dad built a fire in the cooking stove to warm the kitchen before I got up. Sometimes he got me out of my warm bed and cold room. He'd wrap me snugly in a blanket and sit with me close to the open oven door until I felt warm enough to get dressed. After breakfast I was free to play outdoors all day. I would catch and play with frogs and turtles in the ditch or visit four bachelor brothers who lived two alfalfa fields away from us. They would lift me up to ride on their horse's back as he pulled the plow.

On hot days, Mother used an old blanket to make a little playhouse under our quince tree. I spent many happy hours pretending to be a grown-up, cooking mud on a tin pan using a wooden box for my stove and washing dishes in water from the ditch.

On one of these pretend days, Dad stopped by to visit his *vecina* on his way back to the house after hoeing the cornfield. I greeted him warmly and sat him down on an overturned bucket. I served him pretend coffee in a battered tin cup, and said in my broken Spanish, "Forgive me, neighbor, *mi esposo no trabajar.* He used our money to buy a bottle so I can't even serve you beans or a tortilla."

Dad pretended to drink his coffee. Feigning a frown, he shook his head in sympathy. *"¡Tu esposo es muy malo!"* Dad responded as I continued to lament being married to a drinking man.

He later related the story to my mother. They both chuckled over my bold, naive candor, both having faith that Dad's sober period was permanent—that he had finally conquered alcoholism.

When money was available, Mother and Dad travelled to Albuquerque for staples. I waited impatiently for their return, walking up and down the dirt road in front of our house. I knew their purchases would include a bag of candy and flour packaged in a cloth sack. Carefully selected for its flower-print pattern, Mother would use the empty flour sack to sew a blouse or skirt for me.

Life in Corrales was simple. No indoor plumbing, no telephone, no radio. In fact, for a good while, we had no electricity. The seasons were beautiful. Sometimes in the evenings as darkness was approaching, I helped my brother Tony, who often came to stay for a night or two during the summer, gather the cotton that dropped from the huge cottonwood trees in our yard. The adults watched from a distance, as we, the little children in the neighborhood, ran and skipped behind Tony, encouraging him to make interesting trails throughout the dirt yard. When satisfied with his cotton trail making, he would start a fire at one end of the trail. Excited, we followed the fire trail with "ohs" and "ahs" till it ended.

Summer was my favorite season. I spent every possible minute outdoors with the wonderful smells of fresh-cut alfalfa and ripe fruit. Many a time Dad would take out his pocketknife and cut open a watermelon. We would sit alongside the watermelon patch and eat the scrumptious red, juicy pulp to our hearts' content. Families took turns meeting at different homes to pick cherries, shuck corn, stock the pantry with pressure-sealed glass jars, and fill the outdoor food cellar with apples and vegetables. Nothing comes close to the cool, earthy, fruity aroma that hits your senses when you open the door to a dirt cellar filled with fruits and hard vegetables.

In fall and winter, there was butchering and jerky making. Friends gathered to make quilts and share stories. And, of course, there was school. I started my first year of school in a two-room building. For portions of the school day, all ten grades shared the same room. Springtime was for hoeing and planting, for sewing new clothes, and for changing out the winter bedding.

Memories guide our lives. Even when a memory evokes sadness or anger, it gives us strength to reach for something better. On one of my visits to the bachelor brothers' house, I saw the four of them abuse a horse. They had always been so kind and patient with me, though. Three of the brothers had hold of ropes lassoed tightly around the neck of a beautiful, big, black horse. The fourth brother was beating the horse with a long whip as the poor animal bucked high up in the air and whinnied. The stallion's hide was wet from sweat. His braying was an eerie, ear-splitting shrill. His eyes and nostrils were flared with mucus flowing out of his nose. At the time, this was an accepted method of breaking a horse's spirit. I can't erase the sadness I have for this horse nor can I erase the hatred I have for such ignorance.

And then, there are those memories that enrich our lives. As a six-year-old, I remember trudging up a hill carrying a rock the size of a football, pushing my little legs to keep up with Dad's battered 1934 Model B Ford truck. The engine had overheated and water and steam threatened to blow the hood off its hinges. It sounded like a wounded animal gasping for air.

My dad and brother were pushing it up the steep grade of a poorly tarred road. My job was to jam the rock at the base of the rear-right tire when the men stopped to catch their breath. A fuzzy haze of heat lifted from the tarred road. I looked up the road, silently measuring the distance to the top of the hill. I felt my little hands sweating. I remember gripping the rock tightly, fearing I would not be at the rear tire when the men needed to stop. Bubbles on the hot-tarred road raised by the glaring sun snapped and gave way with a spongy feel under my thin-soled shoes.

Finally cresting the hill, the men let the truck come to a standstill. My father reached under the dashboard and pulled out an old greasy rag to protect his hands as he raised the hot metal hood. Heeding his warning to stand back away from the truck, I watched as Dad cautiously unscrewed the radiator cap. Steam bellowed out. Dad left the hood up to allow for faster cooling and waited patiently, knowing it would be some time before the engine was cool enough to fill the radiator with water, which he carried for just such an occasion. We knew that then, and only then, could my brother start the truck and we could continue our journey home.

I remember that both men sat at the edge of the road, still breathing heavily, engrossed in their problem-solving conversation. I was left to wander the sandy roadside hills. I did not feel neglected. I felt exhilarated by my newly found freedom. It was my first experience away from home without my mother. She thought I was too young to make the trip but finally gave in to my pleadings. Even then I was self-assertive and exceedingly independent. It was difficult to convince her that I could take care of myself, but I knew I had won when I saw her smile as I told her that I was now big enough to be of help.

Sitting on a weathered tree stump, not far from my brother and dad, I marveled at the big world around me and about what a lucky, little girl I was. As I turned around to check on the men, I saw my dad pull a worn leather pouch from his hip pocket. From his front pocket he pulled out his pipe. He tapped the bowl of his pipe against the palm of his hand, emptying out the last of the cold, dry ashes. Quite ceremoniously he pressed the tobacco into the bowl to just the right density. He bent his leg to tighten his pants and struck the long wooden match on his thigh, then lit the tobacco accompanied by long drawn-in breaths.

As far back as I can remember, I have loved watching my dad's pipe-lighting ceremony. In the house or outdoors, alone or with neighbors, the routine has been the same. When I was little, he allowed me to fill the pipe, guiding every step of the process, being very particular that the density of the tobacco was packed just right. Sometimes he would even let me hold the lit kitchen match. When my dad was not drinking, he was a patient, peaceful, and shy man.

On this hot day, with the overheated truck, we were on a bartering trip. It took about three hours to travel from Corrales to the little community of Chilili—60 miles from home. Both men rode in the front. I, against their better judgment, rode in the back of the pickup truck with the bushels and boxes of fruit. While sitting on an overturned bucket, wind blowing in my face and my hair flying in every direction, I struggled to stay balanced on my little bucket as the old truck bounced along on the dusty, rutty road. I loved it!

In Chilili, my brother and father would run on ahead of me, knocking door-to-door to present their fruit. After a sale, they returned to the truck to refill their buckets and proceeded knocking on doors while daylight lasted. Cherries, watermelons, and apples were exchanged for pinto beans and, hopefully, some money to use for bills and staples. Occasionally, a receptive customer would come to the door I knocked on and either my dad or brother would come to my aid and negotiate the sale. But mostly, I stayed in the bed of the truck and helped reload the buckets.

The best part of the trip was when Dad brought a buyer to the truck. A bag of pinto beans would be loaded and a bushel of apples or several boxes of cherries removed. All the while, conversation about the weather, the good harvest, the hard times, or about people they knew, would pass between my dad and the buyer. It was especially exciting when my dad referred to me as his "big helper," telling the buyer that he would be lost without my help. I was not aware that my little dress showed stitch marks indicating it had been made from someone's old garment, or that my face was streaked with grime from travelling in the back of the truck, or that my Dad's pants were worn and faded. I was bathed in wealth, surrounded by love and freedom. I was a happy little girl!

At the time of this bartering trip, my parents were in their mid-forties. Together, they had experienced their fair share of hard times. We were hardworking people. We were poor. We were undereducated. Though my dad has always spoken in Spanish, my parents learned to speak, read, and write in both Spanish and English. We were humble and honest in our daily dealings. And we were active Catholics, complying, for the most part, with the dictates of the Church.

Living in Corrales, I had my first real awareness of fear. It was here that my empathy for my mother began. It was here that I first witnessed animal abuse. It was also here that I enjoyed the unity of neighbors who were not my aunts and uncles. I played alone with my imagination as my constant companion, happy in the bountiful country where we lived. Through the protection of childhood, I saw my father and mother busy and happy too.

My father was content to be what and where he was. A bowl of pinto beans for dinner and a peaceful home were enough for him. He never understood why Mother wanted to kill herself working. His favorite sayings to Mother were, "It's God's will," and, "If it was good enough for my mother it should be good enough for you." Years later, Dad said that we were stretching God's patience. He predicted that new inventions would bring about the same devastation that happened at the Tower of Babel. He would say, "If God had wanted us to fly, he would have given us wings."

Mother was not content. She needed change and activity. She needed signs that said we were getting somewhere. Sometimes, after finishing a project or finding a better job, or even while cleaning house, we would hear her say, "Now we're getting somewhere." While Dad was content sitting in the shade, smoking his pipe, watching the world go by, Mother fought the shackles of poverty and ignorance, pushing her family, and mostly herself, to work harder.

Mother's sewing machine was the center of our lives and it was rarely closed. She sewed both for us and for customers. She would pin the pattern to the laid-out fabric, using pins that were gripped in her teeth. After assembling the fabric she lined it up under the lever-foot, turned the wheel and pumped the pedal, making the needle zip along with a steady rhythm, stitching together the pieces of one garment after another.

As for herself, I know she never wore a store-bought garment. Organized and efficient, Mother kept our house in order so that it was welcoming to all who visited. When she was employed away from home, Mother would cover her sewing machine with a linen cloth to keep away any dust. Her machine was sacred. Not a cup of coffee or a child's fingerprint would ever be found on Mother's sewing machine.

For years, Mother's dream was to open a dressmaking shop. From a picture in a magazine, she could create a pattern or change portions of the garment to suit her customers' desires. Never losing sight of her dream, she put aside money and rearranged the living room in anticipation of opening her new business. Ernest constructed a padded wood table for cutting and laying out the fabric patterns. Tony painted a sign: **"Lenore's Sewing Shop."**

But nothing in life is constant, and one day, as quickly as it had appeared, the beautiful oasis in Corrales dried up. I never told anyone about the abuse of the beautiful horse, nor did I ever tell anyone what happened to Mother when Dad's longest period of sobriety came to an end.

# Chapter 19

# DAD STOPPED SMOKING HIS PIPE

E very time Dad started drinking he stopped wearing his hat and smoking his pipe. It was easy to tell when he had fallen off the wagon. This time in Corrales when he started drinking again, he started with a vengeance. I never remember seeing my dad take a drink of alcohol. Maybe the memory is in my subconscious, but I really think Dad hid the physical act from us.

No one ever said Dad was drinking again, but we made signs to each other with our fingers curled in and thumb toward our mouth, indicating that he was back on the bottle. Long before we became aware, Mother knew he was drinking. She became even more obsessed in her determination to free us from the effect of his alcoholism. We spent more private time and, as much as possible, avoided contact with the unkempt, thick-tongued, stumbling idiot who took the place of our kind and contented dad. The intrusion of the drunkard clouded our days.

We accepted Dad's drinking as part of life. My mother did not. She never complained, but you could see her revulsion in the way she looked at him. My reaction to Dad's drinking was to daydream about the good life we would have had if he hadn't been an alcoholic. My older siblings expressed compassion for Dad. They could not bear anyone knowing how their prince turned into a frog.

When Dad started drinking, he stopped working. A dairy farm located beyond the edge of the village of Corrales had an opening for kitchen help. Our mailman offered to give Mother a ride to the farm, which was owned by Congressman Albert Simms and his wife, Ruth. On his delivery route, the mailman dropped Mother and me off at the edge of a tree-lined lane leading to the dairy's main house. Next to the house was a large and impressive private dance and activity hall. Columns supported the overhang of a large beautiful entrance. The ground, as far as my eyes could see, was covered with a velvety, manicured lawn bordered with dazzling flowerbeds.

While mounting the wide porch stairs to the entrance, I was intimidated and awestruck by the magnificent structure and beautiful surroundings. I clung tightly to my mother's hand. I don't know what affect the surroundings had on my mother, but she hesitated at the large door before knocking.

A moment later, the door was opened by a young woman wearing a black dress, starched white apron, and a crown-looking cap on her head. She told Mother to use the kitchen entrance and shut the door in her face. A little stunned but undaunted, Mother headed toward the kitchen entrance where her knock was answered by a large, pleasant woman wearing a white dress nearly covered by her huge white apron. In the crowded kitchen, the woman continued to busy herself with the food cooking on the stove as Mother detailed her capabilities. The woman seemed satisfied with what she heard. She nodded and smiled at my mother. The woman asked Mother what she would do with me while she was working.

"She'll come with me," Mother said unhesitatingly, assuring her that I was obedient and capable of entertaining myself. Apparently the nice cooking woman did not find that agreeable and, therefore, did not hire her.

Walking home, Mother shed silent tears. Her hopes had been crushed. This rejection magnified her desperate situation. But also, I think Mother was crying for me. In her eyes, I too had been rejected. Mother really felt I would not have been a problem. I had been with her on other short-term jobs and I had behaved.

The trek back home was long, hot, and dusty. The ice cream lady peddling her bike toward us was a welcome sight. She sold her frozen products in the village from an insulated box secured to her bike. Mother and this lady had a short conversation about how hard it was to make a living in this community.

"This business," the lady told Mother, pointing to her box, "hardly pays for itself."

Mother expressed her disappointment at being rejected at the dairy, asking the lady if she knew of anyone hiring, emphasizing how desperately she needed to find work. Before we parted, Mother let me select a Popsicle, easing my discomfort while we continued our long walk home.

In need of money, Mother took in ironing for an elderly couple. I remember going with my mother one day to Perea's Tijuana Bar, the local watering hole. She went there to retrieve bed sheets and an iron Dad had taken from our home to exchange for liquor. My eyes took some time to adjust to the dark, smoky, and mostly empty space. A few men were leaning on the bar. A few more were sitting around small tables. All of them turned their heads to stare at the woman and child invading their territory.

Mother walked directly to a large man standing behind the bar. He was very nice and spoke softly to my mother, but insisted she pay for the alcohol my dad had taken before she could retrieve the household items. Mother opened her purse and paid the man, then asked him not to trade liquor for household items with my dad. I don't think he promised to stop. The nice man looked at my mother and shrugged, "Mrs. Sandoval, I'm a businessman."

In retrospect, I am pressed with a lingering regret that we did not protect Mother from my father's alcoholic behavior. After each relapse, full of remorse, maudlin and weepy, Dad let my mother nurse him back to health. And we let her do it alone, with ignorant words like, "If you didn't nag him," "If you watched him," "If you didn't want so much." If, if, if. Mother never attempted to justify herself to us. She simply lifted her load and went on, never letting go of her dreams. Mother never lost sight of her priorities; Dad never found a need to establish any.

By the time of this downward spiral, I had started school. Dad became acquainted with some squalid-looking men who were members of a cult. Addicted to alcohol, this cult professed to worship a fur-covered rock with odd and pathetic rituals. Their rituals included feeding anything metal to this rock which, their creed proclaimed, would give the drunkard superhuman powers. In his drunken state, my otherwise God-fearing, pious father fell under this negative influence. It was the first and only time I saw my dad physically abuse my mother.

Dad had been drinking, pacing, and ranting throughout the day. That night, when we got ready for bed, Mother came into my room and stoked the fire, and added more coal to the pot-belly stove. Mother whispered as she tucked me in, "I am going to sleep with you tonight, Rosabelle." She lay down beside me. Not long after we went to bed, Dad came into the room.

Drunk, disheveled, gurgling, and staggering, Dad continued his delirious raging while he paced the length of the room. His rage reached a boiling point. He pulled Mother off the bed, dragging her across the rough-hewn wood floor to the potbelly stove. I remember her struggling to tuck her long, flannel nightgown down around her legs for decency, but also to avoid the splinters cutting into her skin. Dad grabbed the long-handled shovel used to feed coal to the stove and hit Mother several times with the flat end, accusing her of being the cause of all his suffering.

Dad dropped the shovel and resumed his pacing back and forth, spouting accusations and shaking his finger at my mother lying on the floor. He took no notice of me as I lie huddled in the bed, bewildered and sobbing quietly. After what seemed to be an eternity, his passion subsided. With his arms flailing in all directions and his spent voice dropping in volume, Dad finally left the room.

The beating was out of character. My dad was never aggressively physical prior to this incident. Usually, when drinking, he would preach to the radio, making absurd conversation with the announcer. He would stagger aimlessly around the yard. With his arms raised to the sky he would slam his fist into his open palm, condemning and cursing who knows who. "I am a man of the land!" he would yell. Other times, pacing back and forth in front of Mother while she was sewing, he would spew all sorts of incoherent, angry garbage. He was unpleasant to look at and he had body odor, but I had never seen him hit my mother. For all her married life, Mother had lived through Dad's alcoholism, his drunken verbal abuse, neglect, and irresponsibility. But physical abuse was different— a new wrinkle in their already unstable relationship.

This beating caused a psychological turn in my mother that no one in my family seemed to notice or, if they did, they never mentioned it. She picked herself up off the floor, quietly wiping tears from her face. More with her actions than words, she assured me that everything was going to be all right. She threw a blanket over my shoulders. With flashlight in hand, we walked stealthily into the pitch-black night. We spent the remainder of the night huddled together in the chicken coop hiding from my father.

I do not remember the immediate aftermath of this beating, but it was not long after that we moved to Albuquerque, and I believe Dad went to work in the vegetable fields somewhere in California. My brothers and sisters blamed the move on Mother's restlessness. To my knowledge, Mother never mentioned the macabre episode by the potbelly stove to anyone, not even to her other children.

Yes, mother sold the large adobe house on the three-acre lot that was adjacent to the full-running ditch. She sold the house that was filled with the sweet fragrance of farming—the earthy smells of damp irrigated fields, ripe fruit, and fresh-cut alfalfa. We left the cooperative community of Corrales. We left the church and the handcrafted wood Santo with grotesque features and the villagers' friendly greetings. We left the bachelor brothers and their horse. We left the bend in the road where Dad would build a small fire on cold mornings to fend off the chill as I waited for the school bus. We left the ditch and the land turtle that followed behind me like a pet dog. We left simplicity. We left "paradise right here on earth." And Mother was blamed for our loss. Not one of us realized how trapped Mother was in Corrales with Dad back on the bottle.

I was oblivious to how difficult it was for my mother to move us out of Corrales. I remember the move to Albuquerque as quick and easy. The first two weeks in Albuquerque, Mother and I lived in a two-room apartment located behind a family home.

There was a girl named Geraldine Sanchez who was my same age and lived in the main house. She and I became good friends.

From there, Mother and I moved to a house on the corner of Third Street and Iron Avenue. This house was large enough to accommodate visiting family members and allow Mother to sublet the upstairs. By the time the house in Corrales sold, Mother had found a house to purchase on Sixth Street, in a nice area not far from downtown. My sister Carolyn had married the year before. Because people with Spanish surnames were not encouraged to purchase homes in nicer neighborhoods, my mother had Carolyn's husband purchase the house under his name with the $2,750 down payment, money she had received from the Corrales sale.

In Albuquerque, Mother enrolled me into second grade at Sacred Heart Catholic School. The schooling I had received in Corrales was not up to par with this city school. In the big city, the school curriculum was well defined, and there were many new concepts for me to learn. The nuns were very strict, especially Sister Sheila Marie. I remember her insisting that I print my whole name on one line—*Rosabelle Cecilia Sandoval.* Corporal punishment was still allowed. Hitting a child's palms hard with a wood ruler was a frequent punishment, and the cone-shaped paper "dunce cap" could be freely used to humiliate slow learners. Fortunately, I was a very compliant student and stayed out of the way.

I did get sympathetic attention from all the nuns after Dad visited me one time during school hours. Dad never stayed away long. He soon returned home from California. A student helper came to my classroom to announce that I was wanted in the principal's office. I opened the office door, and saw the principal in utter trepidation. She was standing behind her desk, staring at my dad. I ran to him and as much as I could, put my arms around him. He was quite drunk, smelling badly and looking like a bum. It was not a cold day, but Dad was wearing a dusty green, long army coat that sported a big bulge hiding his bottle. To this day it puzzles me that I was not embarrassed by him. I took his hand and we walked out of the principal's office into the hall. He was very happy to see me. He wanted to know if I had any money. After Dad left, the principal drilled me: Did he live with us? Did my mother work? Did he do this often? Naively and without discomfort, I answered her questions. What more could I tell her? He was my daddy.

**Ernest (left) and Tony (right)
in World War II**

**Leonard in Utah**

*Chapter 20*

# ON THE HOMEFRONT

In 1941, from the radio and newsreels in the movie houses, we in the United States knew about the fighting in Europe. A war threat loomed over America. President Franklin D. Roosevelt and his advisors were divided on whether or not to enter the war in support of our allies. However, when Japan attacked Pearl Harbor, the President prepared the country. During his radio fireside chat of December 9, 1941, he told the American people, *"The attack at Pearl Harbor can be repeated at any*

*one of many points, points in both oceans and along both our coast lines and against all the rest of the hemisphere. It will not only be a long war, it will be a hard war."*

Assembly workers rushed to complete tanks, planes, and ships. Automobile factories converted their shops into airplane engine-building factories, shipyards expanded to begin building warships, and the munitions industry produced greater numbers of weapons and bullets. Fabrication industries hired more people to sew flags, badges, and uniforms. The anticipated needs of an active defense industry also motivated the chemical, rubber, and metal outlets to be prepared.

In the pre-war years, women were not considered part of the American workforce. They were considered homemakers, overlooking the fact that many had always worked outside of the home as nurses, waitresses, domestics, and sales clerks. Equal Employment Opportunity was unheard of. The established system strongly discouraged women's employment in positions a man could fill.

This picture changed when America entered the war. Almost overnight, our men and boys became soldiers and went off to fight. The home front workforce was depleted. Thus creating opportunities in diverse fields of employment for women. Our new workforce exchanged dresses for pants and donned bandanas or helmets. It quickly became apparent that women were highly capable in occupations that heretofore had been male domain. In 1943, women represented sixty-five percent of the workforce, compared to one percent in the pre-war years. Many of my female relatives were willing to be other than homemakers and enthusiastically set out to help when our country called.

During World War II, my brothers, some of my uncles, and many of my cousins fought for our country. I recall the multitude of blue stars hanging in the windows of my relatives' homes. Framed pictures of our boys in uniform and letters read and reread were constant reminders of the boys far away. We were supportive of the war effort and proud of our soldiers. They were our heroes.

While working at the Albuquerque Army Air Base, my sister Carolyn was transferred to Western Chemical Center in Utah. Mother and I went with her. Uncle Frank and Aunt Pritz, bringing my little brother, Leonard, also went to Utah. My vivacious Aunt Pritz was hired as a forklift operator in a munitions factory. Five-foot-two and only one hundred pounds, Pritz also held her own in an assembly line that produced airplane engines.

Mother, resilient and eager to face new challenges, found her work assembling bullets. She needed to know how to multiply and diligently studied to learn her times tables. The industrious women of the day were grateful for the privilege to serve their country and learn a trade. The job opportunities created by the war ameliorated some of the burdens my mother and Aunt Pritz faced. Working in the defense industry helped their financial situation and opened doors for them in a male-dominated society.

Mother not only made good money at the Army depot, but in her spare time she tailored corduroy shirts for the soldiers stationed there. Her new job and the demand for her personalized, custom-made shirts kept her busy. She finally felt she was "getting somewhere" and happily settled into a routine. But we were not long in this progressive mode before Mother received a call from Albuquerque informing her that Dad was in the hospital. His liver was "all but eaten away," the caller said. The prognosis was not good. We left Mother's good job, my school, our relatives and friends, and returned to Albuquerque so Mother could, once again, take care of her husband.

My brother Ernest told me there were times, more so as Dad aged and after an especially heavy drinking bout, Dad was so terrified during his deliriums that he was in danger of hurting himself. Ernest would help Mother tie Dad to the bed. They would monitor his alcohol intake until he stopped trying to get away from his demons. One of the times Dad was admitted into the Veterans Hospital, Mother and I visited him and witnessed Dad slapping the wall and the bed around his body, deranged and heedless of reality.

**Rose (Rosabelle) sixty-five years later
on the steps of Harwood Art Center**

*Chapter 21*

# WATCHING
# THE STARS

In the '40s Albuquerque was a dusty city. When the wind blew you couldn't see in front of you, but most days were sunny. Even in winter, the snow quickly melted. I could always play outside. With me coming from a farming community, the city was exciting, with movie houses, bus transportation, and the freedom to roam. I quickly gained the confidence to ride my bike, Hershey, around town. I carried my Brownie camera in my bike basket and took pictures of people and places that caught my attention.

Riding my bike one day, there it was right in front of me—a beautiful red brick building with grand steps to the entrance. I saw a group of girls standing together on the lawn talking and laughing. At that very moment I knew. This was the place for me. Harwood Girls School was a prestigious boarding facility where girls from other states, even other countries, were sent to learn etiquette and manners along with traditional education.

I pedaled home as fast as I could.

"I want to go to Harwood Girls School," I blurted out to Mother as I dropped my bike on the front doorstep.

**Harwood Girls School then**
**(Photo courtesy Harwood Art Center)**

The very next day, Mother and I walked to the school. As we approached the entrance, Mother adjusted her dress and pushed her short graying locks away from her face, then turned to me. "Stand up straight, Rosabelle."

I pulled my shoulders back and we walked into the building. After an interview with the principal, Mrs. McKeown, I was enrolled under the condition that I would work at the school in lieu of tuition. Nothing could have made me happier.

That evening, holding fabric to my shoulders and measuring, Mother pinned and cut the pieces to begin sewing my new wardrobe. Two weeks later I arrived at the school with my overstuffed suitcase. A senior student greeted me and showed me to my dorm.

Each morning, those of us earning our keep were awakened at 5:30 am. The dorm mother led us to the dining room and instructed us on the proper way to set the tables. After placing the pitcher of water and the glasses on the tables, we went into the kitchen to help with food preparation.

At 7:00 a.m., when the other students came for breakfast, we joined them. A teacher sat at every table to lead us in prayer, making sure we ate all our food. After eating, the main student body was free to leave. It was our responsibility to clear the tables and wash dishes before heading to chapel for a short sermon and a couple of hymns before we were off to class.

We slept in bunk beds—four girls to a room—shy and lacking of privacy, we learned to dress under our covers. We washed our clothes weekly on a scrub board in the basement laundry, hung them on the line to dry. When dry, we ironed them. Our loving, surrogate housemother, Mrs. Anna Fink, mended our clothes and checked under our nails. She affectionately rubbed her hand down our back—actually checking to see that we were wearing our bra. From her we learned the benefits of routine and discipline. And we developed the confidence to be self-sufficient and aware of others.

Once a week after school, we walked ten or more blocks to the YMCA, near Central and Second Street, to take swimming lessons. I wore the swimsuit my mother sewed. I loved to swim and learned to dive, which earned me my Shark Badge. At the end of the day we walked back to the school—hungry—starving, we thought. I would sneak into the kitchen to find dried-out biscuits to share with my friends. On Friday afternoons we were free to relax, catch up on homework or, for those of us who left the premises for the weekend, to pack. Before I could go home for the weekend it was my job to polish the hallway floors with a large commercial machine. The other girls were not able to hold it steady as it oscillated rapidly on the slick tile floor. Being home with my family on weekends kept me from getting lonely.

For our end-of-year party we spent the day at the sand dunes on a bluff overlooking the Rio Grande. We played in the sand, roasted hot dogs, ate s'mores, and sang songs around the open fire long into the evening. The following morning, we packed our bags, said our goodbyes and headed home to spend our summer break with our families.

While school was out, I would ride to Tingley Beach and spend the day in the muddy water, swimming out to the wooden platform and back, honing the skills I had learned at the YMCA. Chilled and out of breath, I would sit on the sandy beach welcoming the hot sun on my sand-covered body. Built during the '30s by diverting water from the Rio Grande, Tingley Beach was really just a large river-water pond with a lifeguard, a floating wooden island, and changing shacks. For a kid in those days, it was the best activity, second only to the dusty roller rink located on the east side of the city.

Sometimes I would ride to the historic Old Town district, where homes in the original settlement of Albuquerque had been remodeled into shops and restaurants around the center plaza. Sometimes there would be a Spanish Fiesta or a band playing on the gazebo in the center of the park. I would make the sign of the cross every time I passed the San Felipe de Neri Catholic Church.

In my youth, far from the hub of the city, the New Mexico State Fair was located on Central Avenue, a section of Highway 66 that continued all the way to California. Once a year, when the Fair came to Albuquerque, I would catch the bus on 4th and Central. Feeling wealthy with two dollars in my pocket, I looked forward to the activities.

Along the bus route, sagebrush dotted the landscape. Sheepherders tended their flocks in the undeveloped area east of Carlisle Boulevard. If I were lucky I might see a rattlesnake or catch a glimpse of a speedy, nocturnal jackrabbit still feeding in the early morning on sprigs of wild grass, sagebrush, and cacti. Their tall ears would catch my attention as they stopped to observe the bus before zigzagging out of view.

Billboards, some in need of refurbishing, lined both sides of Highway 66. Curio shops attracted tourists eager to see snakes in rickety wooden cages, Indian relics, dusty souvenirs, and teepees. A large metal ice chest on the front entrance porch offered cold Coca Cola—a refreshment for travelers after a long drive in the hot car. At the fairgrounds I would spend the day walking through the exhibits, riding every ride on the midway and eating all I could.

I do not remember ever being bored. My girlfriends, Gloria and Wanda, and I would play at each others' homes. Gloria, raised by her elderly parents, once took me to the Soda Dam in Jemez Springs for an outing. One day Gloria, Wanda and I were roller-skating when a fourth girlfriend, Jenny, joined our threesome but she only had one skate. Jenny looked at me and demanded one of my skates. I refused to share. She pushed me, knocking me off balance. I fell. But my brother, Ernest, home from the war, came to my rescue. He picked me up and asked my friends to wait while he took me inside to dry my tears. When I stopped crying, he took me back outside to mend the tiff with my girlfriends. The four of us continued to skate—me on two skates.

My brother Leonard would visit from Taos. He thought I was worldly because of my freedom to roam the city. He and I would slide down the fire escape tube of a two-story building, walk to the railroad tracks to watch the trains, scout for lizards under the viaduct, or climb the big trees on vacant lots, and even peer into the "haunted house" on Fourth Street where an old lady lived alone.

I would take my sister Bea's four-year-old son, Michael Robinson, to see a movie. Mother would give me fifty cents, enough to buy a ticket, a candy bar, and a box of popcorn to share. Once inside, we could watch the same movie over and over again at any one of the theaters my nephew and I picked: Sunshine, Kimo or El Rey. *The Adventures of Ali Baba, Tarzan, Dorian Grey, the Mummy, Snow White and the Seven Dwarfs,* were all fodder for our imagination.

During World War II, POW camps were built throughout the United States. On my bike rides I would pass the Italian prisoners who were held in barracks near the Rio Grande Zoo. These lonely, young men would be standing close to the secure wire fence and yell greetings in Italian to those who passed the area. I did not feel threatened, but I did feel sadness for them. Towards the end of the war, German prisoners were brought in to work on large, irrigated farms plotted along the Rio Grande all the way from Los Lunas to Corrales. And, of course, when the war ended, the prisoners were returned to their homelands.

When my cousin, Felita Sandoval, who was three years older than I, came to visit from

Bernalillo, we liked to walk, talk, and play paper dolls. She told me that if we sprinkled talcum powder on the dolls they would come to life. I believed her—but they never did. At night before bedtime, she and I would climb out of the window of my second story bedroom onto the pitch of the roof, and daydream while watching the stars.

**Rosabelle at about thirteen**

**Lenore and J.I. Sandoval**

*Chapter 22*

# NOW WE'RE GETTING SOMEWHERE

I f Albuquerque opened new vistas for me, it also opened new vistas for Mother. She found work to sew fiesta dresses for a shop on Central Avenue, not far from our home. One day, unsatisfied with the progress the crew had made in his absence, her employer picked up a bundle of cut fabric and threw it at my mother. She caught the stack, threw it back at him and walked off the job, leaving everyone with mouths agape.

My mother continued to work for that company from her home, and under her conditions. I remember pulling the bottom thread to gather long strips of fabric so she could assemble the multi-tiered colorful fiesta skirts. When friends stopped by, Mother would keep working. "Come in. Come in, there's hot coffee on the stove," she would say, lifting her chin toward the kitchen and pointing with puckered lips. "Bring the biscochitos from the cupboard and sit here by me while I work."

A couple of times a year, Mother and I would take a trip to Taos. We travelled by bus, taking two suitcases—one for our clothes and the other crammed full of neatly folded items: special occasion blouses, skirts, baby clothing and bonnets, baptismal and holy communion dresses, aprons, and potholders she had made to sell to family and friends. We walked to the different houses. Mother carried the neatly-packed second suitcase. Occasionally, Mother would have to stop to discreetly pull the sag out of her stockings. Everyone greeted us warmly, and Mother's sewn efforts were carefully considered and selected. When we left, Mother reached for a nickel from her purse to give to the little nephews and nieces we met in the yard. She would touch their faces and tell them how good they were or how pretty they looked.

There was always laughter and news to share. One time I remember my aunt telling my mother that the ranch in Rayado where we used to live had been given to the Boy Scouts of America. In fact, quite generously, Waite Phillips and his wife had given 127,000 acres of fertile grazing and mountain land, which included herds of sheep, goats, bison, cattle, and horses, to the Scouts for training and development of young men. Most important to me, on that land was the converted tack room and the little mound where I took my excitingly dangerous stroller ride down the hill. It made me sad to hear I would never see our little house again.

Sometimes while in Taos, Mother would leave me with an aunt so she could travel to Cimarron to visit relatives. Mother would walk from my cousins' house the lengthy distance along the dusty, unpaved road to visit her mentor. Mother told me that Mrs. Springer was always happy to see her and greeted her warmly. Charles Springer had passed away in 1932. Thin and aging, Mrs. Springer was living in the pump house, the only building left standing after the fire burned the mansion. She had converted this stone structure into a one-room efficiency, sparsely furnished, clean and comfortable. The two women chatted about the present happenings in their lives, taking time to reminisce about the past. Mrs. Springer always hugged Mother and invited her to visit more frequently.

The last time Mother visited Mrs. Springer at the pump house, the elderly gray-haired woman was wearing rubber boots and feeding a few sheep on what had once been the lush, carefully manicured lawn surrounding the mansion. Only rubble covered the ground where the beautiful rose garden once grew. Mother said Mrs. Springer's face had a hollow appearance and that she seemed to have aged years before her time. It was very sad for my mother to see her mentor in such a compromised state.

Mrs. Springer's affinity for my dad endured until her death. Eva, Mother's long-time friend, wrote to Mother about Mrs. Springer's passing, telling her that just before Mrs. Springer died she was calling for "Fonzie."

After reading the letter, Mother sat down and cried. Throughout the years, Mother's endearment for the woman who had provided her security, happiness, and many valuable life lessons had not waned. Mother would frequently reminisce, telling me about the songs and stories and fashions and personalities that she came in touch with through her relationship with Mrs. Springer.

Mother was not one for showing emotion, but sometimes when talking about the years at the Springer Mansion she would stare out the window as if staring at a faraway place. Her eyes would gloss over and she would say, "I wish those days had never ended."

Over the years, my parents have shared stories with me about their novel experiences at the Springer Ranch, about the beautiful rose garden Dad had planted and how much my mother loved it. Both had warm memories of the special consideration they had received from Charles and Mary Springer. Mother and Dad witnessed the end of an era—an era that taught them a new way of thinking.

I was never in the Springer Mansion, nor did I ever meet Charles and Mary. It was many years ago that my parents worked there, and my search has failed to pinpoint the exact location where it once stood. I know that death is inevitable, and yet a yearning hovers over me—a longing to walk the wood floors of the mansion and see the fresh roses in their vases.

# Chapter 23

# ¿QUE PASA, LINDA, ESTÁS SOLA?

I was only eight years old the first time I returned to Taos on my own. I had convinced my parents I was old enough—or they knew I was not going to take no for an answer. I set off on my journey, baby doll and suitcase in hand. I had purchased a round trip ticket to Santa Fe not knowing it would not get me to Taos. After realizing the bus I was on was headed back to Albuquerque I notified the driver that I was on the wrong bus. He nodded and wheeled the Greyhound off the pavement and onto the dirt at the outskirts of Santa Fe. After I identified my suitcase, he removed it from the compartment and placed it on the ground near where I was standing on the side of the road. He closed the compartment hatch and, without a word, the driver disappeared into the bus. He closed the door, shifted gears, and stepped on the gas, leaving me in a cloud of exhaust.

While holding my doll and her blanket, I watched the bus get smaller and smaller. I looked in both directions and saw an occasional car pass by, but no one to ask for help. I sat down on my suitcase and started to cry. I was aware my dilemma was serious, but I was most anxious to prove I was capable of handling my freedom.

Three men driving north noticed me and made a U-turn, stopping their old car close to where I was sitting. All three men got out of their car and walked slowly toward me.

"What are you doing out here all by yourself?" The tallest man asked.

"I want to go to Taos, but the bus went the wrong way."

Looking at each other, they chuckled.

The tall man said, "We can't take you to Taos, but we can drive you back to the bus station." He put my suitcase in the trunk while another took my hand. My other hand held the doll and blanket. Without hesitation I sat in the back seat with this nice man, and the four of us retraced my route back to the bus depot.

Elated and my confidence restored, I walked into the station and straight to the ticket counter.

"The next bus to Taos doesn't leave until eight o'clock in the morning, young lady," the man at the ticket counter said to me.

I stepped back dazed. Neither the place I left nor the place I was going to had a phone. I sat on an unpadded hardwood bench and, for the second time, the tears came.

Asking for help did not cross my mind and searching for a solution only intensified my desperation. Fear was not the issue. I neither considered that I could be in trouble with my parents nor did I consider the possibility I could be in harm's way—I just wanted to get to Taos.

Between arrivals and departures, the Santa Fe Bus Station was relatively empty. Time passed slowly and tearfully. Still holding my doll, I used her blanket to wipe my face as I took in my surroundings. The activity in the station increased as another bus arrived. An elderly couple, who looked a little like my aunt and uncle, caught my attention as they walked into the station with their daughter. While passing by my bench, the family took notice of my teary face and stopped.

"*¿Que pasa, linda? ¿Estás sola?*" their daughter asked.

I held back tears explaining my situation, beginning with when I left Albuquerque and adding that the Taos bus would not leave until morning. The three expressed concern and promised to come back after they bought their daughter's ticket. When they returned, their daughter sat next to me and suggested I sleep in her bed that night, explaining that she was now headed back to Albuquerque.

"You'll have my room to yourself, *linda*."

"We will walk you back to catch your bus in the morning," her father offered.

What an adventure! While walking to their house, the woman held my hand and her husband carried my suitcase. They asked about my parents and where I lived. I responded, half in Spanish, half in English, to their questions.

Their humble, spotlessly clean home, with linoleum floors and homemade cotton curtains tied back to show lace sheers, was a replica of the many houses I knew in Taos. Suddenly I felt hungry. Leaving my belongings near the entrance door, I followed the kind lady into the kitchen.

*"En tu casa estas, Rosabelle,"* she said, making me feel at home.

She retrieved a cloth from a nearby white metal cabinet. I washed my face at the kitchen sink where a curtain hung on a string to hide the plumbing. We talked while she prepared a meal. Shortly after eating, though, it was bedtime. The bedspread in their daughter's bedroom was folded back. I climbed into comfort, feeling like a princess in a fairy tale.

The next morning I awoke with the smell of freshly baked bread. The lady helped me brush my hair and while making my bed she told me stories about her daughter when she was little. I was treated to a piece of hot, fresh bread with jelly and a glass of milk. My kindhearted hosts walked me to the station, telling me on our way how happy they were I had stayed with them. Euphoric, well rested, and eager to continue my journey, I boarded the eight o'clock bus. A couple of hours later, I arrived in Taos, safe and sound.

As incredulous as this story might appear, it is to the best of my recollection, a factual account of my first independent journey. Neither my dear parents nor the relatives in Taos ever heard this story. It would have worried my parents and cast doubt on my reputation of being capable and independent.

Carrying my suitcase, my doll and her blanket tucked under my arm, I walked around the plaza a couple of times checking out familiar places and basking in my freedom. How happy I was to be in Taos! A few men sat on the plaza wall. For the most part, though, the plaza was empty. The hardware store and the five-and-dime were closed, but the Soda Shoppe was open. I thought to stop but quickly decided to keep moving. It was a quiet Sunday and satisfied with my sightseeing, I headed to my aunt's house.

I passed by the Catholic Church and the vacant schoolyard and started down the short hill to get to Martinez Lane. The road was littered with loose rocks. I stumbled, pitting my knees with sand and grit. My doll landed on the dirt. I picked her up and brushed off the dirt from the dress my mother had made for her. Bruised and scraped knees were not a problem for me. I continued walking past the familiar, settled adobe houses with flowering, potted geraniums sunning on windowsills. At the edge of a hard-packed dirt yard I stopped to marvel at the yellow blossoms covering a Rosa de Castilla bush. My memory flashed back to when we lived on La Loma and watching my mother sprinkle water from a small pan with her hand to hold the dust down before sweeping our dirt yard.

*"Rosabelle, it's getting dark. You need to come in."* The memory of my mother's voice causes me to miss her.

I reached to touch the fuzzy leaves hanging low on the trees. Crystal clear water drew my attention. I stopped at the little canal to study the spider-like bugs darting on the surface. Everywhere, hollyhocks were in bloom. The exhilaration of freedom magnified my endearment of this wonderful place where I was born, and flooded me with memories of the past.

As I continued down the lane, someone came out of an outhouse. I remembered how my cousin and I got into trouble when we were little. Loyola and I were giggling in the outhouse, kneeling on the seat trying to aim into the opening like boys do.

Tia Eustacia yelled, *"¿Qué estás chicas traviesos haciendo? Get out of there!"*

We both got a pat on the behind. I do not remember any other time that I felt discomfort in the presence of my kind aunts.

After arriving at Tia Josefina's house, I walked up the porch steps and knocked on the screen door. My heart leapt as I saw my aunt through the screen sitting at her kitchen table. All of my aunts are unique and special people and all have had a great influence on my life. However, my favorite aunt has always been Tia Josefina.

She came to the door wearing her Sunday dress, and called out my name. "Rosabelle!"

She bent down to pull me close, and hugged me tightly. I kissed her cheek and noticed her hair had been flattened by her hat.

"Come in, come in, Rosabelle. Are you hungry?" Tia Josefina asked. "Did you really come by yourself? How is your mother?"

While we sat at the kitchen table, we continued our question and answer game. Smiling at my clumsy Spanish, my aunt reached for her apron hanging on a hook near the stove. With a potholder to protect her hand, she used an iron poker to lift the lid of the wood-burning stove and inserted a couple of sticks from the bin. She made some dough. Holding a freshly rolled-out tortilla, she checked the heat by circling her open hand a few inches above the stove's surface. It was not long before I was eating warmed beans with red chile and a scrumptious hot tortilla with butter.

For about five years of my childhood I visited Tia Josephina in the summer and played with my cousins. Dressing paper dolls and playing house with Loyola, my cousin who lived with

Grandmother Gertrudes, was fun. But I was a tomboy. So wearing a large towel clipped around my neck, jumping off walls to fight a war as Army Commandos, or sporting a holster and guns at my waist pretending to be cowboys and Indians was far more exciting. Norberto, Tia Josephina's son, was the leader who dramatized our actions, but I kept up with him.

When there wasn't someone to play with, I could visit my aunts on Martinez Lane. They were always so kind to me. At my Aunt Josephina's house I chopped wood. One day I broke the axe handle. I walked to the hardware store carrying the axe head and bought a new handle. After returning to my Tia's house, I proudly repaired it by hammering a nail into the top of the handle to secure it to the iron head. I then continued to chop wood. I spent my entire vacation each year with bruised knees, swollen knuckles, and muddy shoes. I loved every moment.

My cousins were older than I. As the years rolled by they were no longer willing to play with me. They were growing up. Their need to find work and girlfriends interfered with our summer freedom. It was at the end of World War II and work for young men was scarce.

Some of my cousins were encouraged to go to Boys Town in Nebraska. Started as a home for orphaned boys, my cousins were lucky to have been accepted as 'hardship cases' due to the strained economic conditions in Taos.

I, too, was growing up. And, alas, my independent summer visits to my birthplace, regretfully, came to an end.

# Chapter 24

# THERE ARE
# NO BAD BOYS

During the difficult economic depression and war years, employment opportunities in Taos were even more limited than they were across the country. Young men were especially at a loss for work. Domestic chores and menial jobs helping a relative did not pay nor properly prepare them for employment, had they been able to find work. Idle time lead to boredom and the opportunity to get into trouble.

Talking to his mother, Epifanio, my cousin, begged her to let him quit school. Not knowing how to counter his request, Tia Fedelina asked the parish priest for help. He suggested Boys Town as a possible solution for her son.

Father Edward J. Flanagan, a parish priest in Ireland, moved to America to work in the Diocese of Omaha, Nebraska. Actively involved with his new parish, he witnessed orphaned, neglected boys roaming the streets, getting into trouble. His concern for these boys motivated him to establish an orphanage based on his idea that, "There are no bad boys. There is only bad environment, bad training, bad example, bad thinking." However, convincing the Diocese to fund the project was not easy. Refusing defeat, he sought the aid of local businesses and secured the use of a run-down Victorian mansion. Boys Town started with four boys.

Boys Town pioneered new concepts that emphasized social preparation. It became a model for boys' homes worldwide. At one time, their logo was a picture of a boy carrying a younger boy with the caption reading, "He ain't heavy, he's my brother."

Through the Taos priest's efforts and with my aunt's encouragement, Epifanio and Billy, his brother, enrolled into Boys Town. This opened the door for other Taos boys to attend, changing the course of their lives. My Uncle Alex was a member of the Boys Town Choir, active in sports, and while there, improved his guitar playing skills.

Billy and a friend were lonely after being away from home for a few weeks and decided to run away from Boys Town. Packing their meager belongings and peanut butter sandwiches, they started walking, heading back to Taos. They walked southwest for miles and stopped to rest. My cousin had doubts about leaving the school. He wanted to return, but his friend did not. The friend continued to walk, leaving Billy alone in the park to contemplate his next plan of action.

It did not take his friend long to realize what an enormous trek lay ahead of him. He returned to the park, grateful to find Billy still sitting there. The boys found a police station where an officer called Father Flanagan. On the trip back to the school, the officer treated the young boys to a restaurant meal and encouraged them not run away again.

Arriving at the school, Father Flanagan met them and thanked the officer, paying him for his effort. Taking the boys into his office, he asked what they would need to make them want to stay in school. One wanted to learn to play an instrument and the other wanted to play football. Chatting with the boys, he took the opportunity to reinforce what the school could offer them. Father Flanagan called the coach and music instructor and arrangements were made to fulfill the boys' wishes. Thus, they continued their education at Boys Town.

Father Flanagan was born July 13, 1886 and died on May 15, 1948. Boys Town alumni from Taos travelled to Omaha to attend the funeral services. Dignitaries and students from around the world attended. The funeral procession was so long that cars were still leaving the school, some ten miles away, as the hearse carrying the body was arriving at the church.

*Chapter 25*

# WALKING OVER OBSTACLES

My mother was just less than five feet tall with fair skin and black curly hair, but by the time I knew her, her hair was turning gray. Her pleasant, wholesome demeanor made her attractive. It may be that all girls wish they looked like their mother. I always have. Though Mother had definite principles, she also had a wonderful sense of humor. I remember many times laughing with her till it hurt too much to laugh anymore.

Once, when we were visiting Mother, Ernest was attempting to prove a raw egg could not be broken squeezing it from the oblong position. Five of us were crowded into the small kitchen arguing the possibilities of the egg, while Mother made her way around us as she cooked. Everyone held their breath as Ernest squeezed the egg. Suddenly the eggshell burst, spewing its contents directly onto Mother's hair. Yolk and clear slime dripped from her curly, gray strands.

Our jaws dropped as we looked at Mother. She wheeled around. "Ernest, why did you do that to me?" she said in shock and left the kitchen to wash her hair. But under her breath we could hear her suppressed giggles. Mother returned a few minutes later, wiping tears of laughter from her eyes, reigniting our hilarious reaction. Still laughing, my sisters and I cleaned the mess. As always, we sat down to enjoy Mother's prepared food.

We sometimes found ourselves laughing when Mother did not appreciate being the brunt of our humor. One spring day, while raking and clearing debris to create a flowerbed, Mother said to my brother, "Tony, move this dirt-filled wheelbarrow to the pile in the back yard."

Tony, play wrestling with cousin Monjo who was visiting us from Taos, responded, "In just a minute."

"Mother was too impatient," Tony told me. "She grabbed the handles on the wheelbarrow to move it herself. The strain of lifting broke the elastic band on her homemade bloomers. I looked up just in time to see them drop around her ankles in a puddle."

He chuckled and continued, "Without missing a beat, she walked over her bloomers, straining to push the heavy wheelbarrow in front of her with Monjo and me bent over in uncontrollable laughter. 'Wait, Mother, I'll get it.' I told her, taking the wheelbarrow from her to move the dirt."

"Mother turned sharply, bent down and picked up her bloomers and walked briskly toward the house. She wasn't laughing. . . but Monjo and I couldn't stop laughing."

Tony seemed to present more challenges for Mother than the rest of us. Mother and I were washing dishes one evening when Tony came into the kitchen. Carrying a new pair of pants, he asked Mother to alter the pockets to make them wider and deeper. It was the end of the day and she was tired.

"Tomorrow, Tony." Mother said. "Leave them on the sewing machine."

But Tony persisted. "I can't wait till tomorrow, Mom. I need them tonight!"

Mother dried her hands and took Tony's trousers over to her new electric sewing machine. After pinning fabric to the existing pockets, Mother snapped the presser-foot down, guiding the edges as she gently pressed the pedal. With the steady rhythm of the sewing machine clicking away, she neatly seamed the new larger pockets to the inside of Tony's new pants. Tony waited impatiently for Mother to finish. She turned the pants right side out again and shook them into shape. Mother handed the altered pants to my brother. Tony went into the bedroom and changed. He came out of the room adjusting each pant leg down over his boots. He confidently tucked his shirt in, slipped his wallet into his back pocket, and his knife and truck keys into his new front pockets. For a moment he was silent.

"What?" My mother asked.

Hunching over, Tony reached deep into his pockets, all the way to his knees, and retrieved his knife and keys, bringing with them the inside of both pockets that now hung outside his pants like the ears of a hound dog.

Recognizing how humongous she had made his pockets, Mother leaned forward, breaking into a hysterical laughter. "What's the matter with my head?" she said.

I don't remember if Mother fixed the mistake right away, but I do remember that Tony did not share my mother's amusement.

Though, I suppose, I presented my mother with a bucketful of fretful challenges myself. The last time Mother and I were in Utah I met the man who would become the father of my five children. I literally saw stars when he said hello to me. He was nineteen and the most handsome man I had ever seen. He was taking flying lessons at the time and would circle his plane over the school grounds tipping the wing of the Piper Cub as I waved back excitedly.

We had only dated a short time before we heard North Korea had invaded South Korea. He enlisted in the National Guard. Upon receiving orders that he would be stationed at a military base in Kansas, he proposed to me. He planned to leave me with his family in Kansas City, Missouri. It was there we married, in a small chapel, with his mother as our witness. It was just a few months after my sixteenth birthday when I said, "I do."

During his leave from duty, we made a trip to Albuquerque. All my family gathered at Mother's house to meet my husband, Gerald Spader. Ignoring the charming, statuesque man beside me, my sister Bea looked me up and down. "So..." she said, referring to my tomboy personality, "You just climbed down from the tree and got married?"

While my brothers took my husband out for a drink to welcome him into the family, I rolled up my jeans and played a game of stick baseball with my nephews. That evening, Carolyn helped Mother prepare dinner, while Bea and I tended to her baby.

A few days later as my husband and I were loading the car to return to Kansas City the family came outside to say goodbye. I hugged my sister Bea. She candidly said to me, "Rosabelle, how did *you* catch such a good-looking man?" Mother, hugging me tightly, brushed tears from her eyes and we were on our way.

Mother lived her life zealously, determinedly walking over obstacles. There were times between the happy commotion and her fatigue that she would sew a sleeve on backwards or make a mistake that gave her an opportunity to turn fabric into an apron instead of a blouse. Mother's reaction to such mishaps would be a deep sigh. Scolding herself, she would say, "Tsk, tsk, I don't know what's the matter with my head."

If we suggested she lie down because she was not feeling well, she would say, "I can be sick lying in bed, or I can be sick getting work done." It was Mother's presence that made our home warm and comfortable. More times than not, the house would be congested with friends, relatives, or both, all talking and laughing, indulging in the hearty meals she cooked and served.

Mother dropped her personal goals, not only to take care of Dad and her family, but her relatives as well. A cousin pregnant out of wedlock waiting for her baby, an uncle unable to find work, cousins starting out in the big city, relatives visiting from another state—all came when they needed a place to stay and all were accommodated. When she had an unoccupied room, Mother rented that portion of the house to bring in money. Those tenants, too, became part of the family, affectionately referring to her as "Mom." She helped raise two grandsons, and at one time or another she had one or more of her adult children living with her. Through it all, she maintained her balanced demeanor and created a safe haven for all.

Although I didn't understand at the time, the talk and commotion that filled Mother's house was psychologically beneficial for her. Work and involvement kept her free of worry, sadness, and self-pity. She could function with multiple tasks at one time and disengage herself from a drinking husband or a son far away. The good therapy benefited all of us. We enjoyed and participated happily, assuming it our natural right, unaware of the effort it demanded from her.

I grew up knowing she loved me the most—so did each of my siblings. Mother, unhampered by petty possessiveness and comparisons, had the ability to make each of us feel very right about ourselves and very important to her. We loved her and showed our affection, but we never took notice of her personal desires.

It was on a Friday when I was visiting that she experienced a painful cramp on her way to the bathroom. A sharp pain overtook her and she fell across the kitchen table moaning, unable to move. I was finally able to persuade her to visit a doctor. I searched the Yellow Pages to find a doctor within walking distance from her home who would see us that same day. She took off her apron, freshened her face and on a beautiful autumn day, she and I walked to his office.

We waited for the doctor in a small room, scantily furnished with cheap, badly worn leather chairs, dog-eared magazines, and bare wood floors. A nurse showed us to a small room and helped Mother onto a metal examining table covered with a rollout paper sheet. I stood near her. In only a few minutes the doctor came through the door walking slowly. He was old and looked very tired. After introducing himself he took my mother's pulse and listened to her heart. He paid attention to her timid complaints of constant fatigue, the pain in her midsection, and the pain in her back. Within a few minutes the doctor had evaluated her and the examination was over. He told her to get more rest and to expect such discomforts with her advancing age. She was sixty-seven. She and I wanted to believe that nothing was wrong.

On Sunday, like many previous Sundays, I walked with my children to Mother's house, ready to attend Mass. Dressed and ready for church, Mother said, "I don't feel like going to Mass today."

I made coffee and she and I sat in the small living room. I sent the children out to play and Mother lay back on the daybed.

"Play the piano for me, Rosabelle," she said.

I did.

*Chapter 26*

# MÉDICOS, CURANDERAS AND BRUJAS

When I was a small child in the modest community of Taos, life was simple but harsh. Medicine was herbs, *medicos, curanderas,* even witchcraft. Our superstitions made us leery of conventional medicine. Food was fried in rendered lard. Our clothing was homemade. We were poor, undereducated, and secluded, without the benefit of television and radio or accessible newspapers and magazines. Friends and relatives who visited our home, few educated above primary grades, were the role models of my early education. Books were a rarity, but the Catholic Missal, printed in Spanish, was found in most homes.

Frequent visitors enjoyed coffee and biscochitos or hot tortillas with chokecherry jam at our heavy wooden kitchen table while Mother continued to cook or sew. They all laughed, recounting silly pranks. Or they cried and received sympathy for their hardships. They worried about the weather and the sick neighbor. They talked about God's judgment and argued with their different interpretations of the priest's Sunday sermon. They gossiped about the people who missed Mass. They shared stories about cures and *brujas*, about husbands, and about their painful experiences of childbirth. I believed all that I heard. Husbands and hardships did not grab my attention, but witches and strange healing methods perked my ears, and I would stop playing to listen.

Young and impressionable, my mind was like a sponge. Visions of hospitals were nebulous and illusionary. They were mystical places on the scary side of my thinking—the side where I thought of prisons or of the chaos at the end of the world. I wondered and worried about burning in hell if I disobeyed my parents. I really wondered about where the people were put when they "got crazy," about the highly infectious tuberculosis disease and the patients who were quarantined and confined to sanitariums. A visit to the doctor for a cold or a high fever, or even an earache, was not routine. Only the very sick consented to a doctor's examination.

In the days of my youth, children's ability to reason was not recognized or protected. I listened, open-mouthed, to stories told and retold of a friend in an insane asylum. The storytellers believed herbs and ancient cures could combat illness better than doctors. They talked of spells that could cause a mother's milk to sour or bring pestilence or drought upon the crops in the field. We were suspicious of anyone who was overly attentive to a newborn. We theorized the attention would bring about the curse of the "The Ojo." If the baby became sick shortly after the visit, a *medica* would visit the home and remove the curse of the "Evil Eye."

Superstition, *brujas*, and *curanderas* were a part of life. If a black cat walked in front of you, if you walked under a ladder, or if the weather was bad on your wedding day, bad luck would follow. If an expectant mother accidentally looked at the full moon, even for a mere moment, the moon would consume the baby. I remember listening to our neighbor's tales of how she saw Doña Eufelia, dressed in black garments, fly above the roof of her house. It was said she lost her eye during one of her mystical spells when she turned herself into a dog and was beaten by mean spirits. Some of the adults and I believed that she could turn herself into a ball of fire.

Stories like these were the topic of conversation whenever adults gathered to share a meal, sew quilts, make tamales, or just visit over a cup of coffee. Unlike the people in Salem, who convicted and burned suspected witches, we did not ostracize or convict them in my little village. We only talked about them, and like the residents of Salem, believed they existed. Such stories gave me goosebumps. The fact that these supernatural powers were never discussed in Doña Eufelia's presence was natural to us. In our daily life she was a kind, elderly woman mingling comfortably with her neighbors.

Mother grew up with insight into magical medical practices, commonly believed to be sorcery. My wise mother put little stock in *brujas* and the stories she heard about them. But she did have faith in a cup of strong, bitter, black chaparral herb tea to cure the pain in her back and the knot in her stomach, denying the fact that her pain was getting worse.

*Chapter 27*

# LENORE

## IN THE BLINK OF AN EYE

Today is December 16, 1963. I am twenty-eight years old. The cold and gray winter clouds hang low over the mountaintops as I retrieve the newspaper from the driveway. I scuff my shoes on the front doormat as I read the headlines reminding me our country is still mourning the loss of our 35th President. While pouring my day's first cup of coffee, the phone rings. ...

"Hello?"

I hear my father's slurred speech. *"Rosabelle, llamaron de Taos."*

"Dad, what's wrong?" I ask, sensing his anxiety.

*"Lenore esta en el hospital. Qué crees que deberíamos ¿ir a Taos?"* Dad asks, suggesting we all go to Taos together. Even now, with his wife in the hospital, he is on one of his alcoholic binges. It's difficult to show him sympathy when he is drinking.

After hanging up the phone, I call my brothers and sisters. We make quick arrangements to drive to Taos. I pity my father. We refuse to take him with us. The last thing Mother needs now is her drunken husband. My thoughts are with her, and I cannot worry about my dad.

As we pass through Santa Fe, I stare out the window at the place where the bus dropped me off and left me by myself in the middle of nowhere. Though I no longer remember their names, for a moment I recall the three men who gave me a ride back to the bus station so many years ago. As we wind through the canyon along the Rio Grande, the scenic road between Santa Fe and Taos takes me back to a time when I was just a little girl moving to Corrales in Uncle Alex's big, stinky, wobbly, bouncing, old truck. I remember the Mason jar with river water, my mother's torn stocking, Dad breaking down the gate, so eager to greet my mother.

Jarred back into reality, we arrive at the Holy Cross Hospital in Taos. The nurse at the desk is aware of our mother. Her compassionate look is disconcerting. She informs us Mother is with the doctor and directs us to the congested ICU waiting room.

A small television turned on without sound, hangs from the ceiling. The combined smell of medicine and disinfectant permeates my nose.

Ernest looks at Carolyn. "Did you call Leonard?"

Carolyn nods. "There was no answer."

Lost in our own thoughts, we sit quietly in the cold, sterile room. How could we not have realized Mother was so sick? We should have been more aware and concerned for her. How could we not have recognized how serious her condition had become?

Carolyn stands up and looks out the window. Turning to us, she breaks the silence. "Mother can't stay in this hospital. We need to take her back to Albuquerque."

No one responds.

I get a whiff of cigarette smoke as Tony eases himself down on the chair next to me. He leans close and whispers, "What's taking so long?"

Putting my hand on his, I kiss his cheek and respond, "I don't know."

Ernest, pacing and unable to sit still, says, "This waiting is too much for me." He leaves the room to get coffee, asking us to call him immediately if we hear anything. Fear of the unknown grips all of us. A crying baby draws my attention. I watch as her mother patiently tries to soothe her.

Ernest returns a short time later. Finally, a nurse heads in our direction. She tells us the doctor has finished his examination, and Mother is being transferred back to her room. "You can see her in ten to fifteen minutes," she says.

As we walk into Mother's room, she acknowledges each of us with a smile. She apologizes for the trouble she feels she is causing. In the week since she left Albuquerque, she has dwindled to half her normal size. I recall the last time I spoke with Mother. It was a week before, and she was leaving for Taos. Pale and weak, she sat in the back seat of my uncle's car. I put a blanket over her legs and kissed her cheek. I wanted to beg her not to go but she was determined to go to Taos to see a *curandera.* When she arrived in Taos, Mother's relatives, alarmed by her pallor and lack of energy, convinced her to see a doctor. Only when all her herbal efforts failed did she consent to their wishes.

Now, lying very still in her bed, she expresses no discomfort, but I know she is in pain.

Carolyn asks, "How do you feel, Mother?"

Mother smiles weakly and closes her eyes.

A long, clear plastic tube hangs down from a bottle, releasing fluid through a needle inserted and taped to the top of Mother's small hand. So weak, so fragile, my mother is wan and resigned. Looking at her lying on the hospital bed, half swallowed up by the light blanket, I truly understand the meaning of the phrase, "having the rug pulled out from under you."

The nurse informs us that the doctor will be in shortly. She checks my mother's pulse and increases her pain medicine. Mother thanks the nurse, who bends down and kisses my mother on the forehead. Mother's eyes close. We wait for the doctor. Again and again, it amazes me how my mother brings out the best in everyone. In some mysterious charismatic way, she transmits a comforting peace and acceptance.

Standing by the side of Mother's bed, I hold her warm hand. The lines on Tony's face have deepened since this morning. Fettered and confused, he sits down in a chair in the corner of the small room.

The doctor enters Mother's room and places his hand on her wrist, checking her pulse. "Is that pain medicine working for you, Mrs. Sandoval?"

Mother smiles—it must be working, or she has resolved not to show her discomfort.

Mother closes her eyes and the doctor turns to us, tipping his head toward the door. We follow him out of her room and into an empty room down the hallway. He introduces himself. With his hands jammed deep into his white coat pockets, he collects his thoughts. Speaking softly, he directs his attention to my older sister, Carolyn. She is all but levitating with the importance bestowed upon her by the doctor's attention. I am grateful, however, that Carolyn's emotions are sufficiently intact to understand what the doctor is saying. My head is in a thick fog, too thick to grasp the doctor's words.

"There is nothing more we can do for your mother. The cancer is so widespread, we can't even tell where it started." He continues, addressing all of us. "I'm very sorry. I wish there was something we could do. Nothing known to man can help your Mother now."

The doctor shifts his weight back and forth. He puts his hand on Ernest's shoulder, and looks around the small room at each one of us. "She has indicated to me that she does not want to stay in the hospital. Take her home and make her comfortable. Ease her pain as much as you can."

We remain silent.

"Your mother is a remarkable woman!" The doctor says and leaves the room.

Carolyn announces, "I will take Mother to my house."

I don't agree but I cannot respond. My mind floods with memories: *Crimson-red water, the sign "Lenore's Sewing Shop," her hands on a piece of fabric running it past the needle of her treadle sewing machine, the sound of her laughter, her small steps against Dad's long strides.*

*My senses have taken leave. I move and I function, but I experience no normalcy. I experience nothing. In a strange vacuum I can use my five senses without feeling. My eyes work, but I don't see. I want to protest, but my voice is gone. I am far away. I can't hear and I can't feel. Tears are rolling down my face so I must be crying. I am in a strange place. Of course, I am dreaming! I can't live without my mother.*

Somewhere far away, I hear Tony trying to soothe me, "Don't feel so bad, Rosabelle, everything is going to be okay."

How do people live without their mother— the essence of life? Blinking my eyes and shaking my head I try to clear my thoughts. How will *I* live without my mother? I have never considered the reality of my mother's death. Thoughts of my children come into my mind and quickly fade. Only disconnected, cloudy thoughts rattle around in my head. I can only compose myself enough to go back to my mother's room to hold her warm hand.

I whisper, "Mother." But she does not respond.

I try to remain calm for her.

Ernest and Bea enter Mother's room. Grief overcomes my oldest sister. Ernest steps near to Mother's bed. He tries to speak but is unable. His face crumbling, he leaves the room. Mother's eyes remain closed.

Minutes later, after gaining his composure, Ernest returns to plead with Mother. "I want you to stay with us. We can take care of you."

She does not respond.

Knowing she would rather return to her own home, he offers, "Then I'll go stay with you at your house."

"I'll be less trouble to Carolyn...I don't want to burden you," Mother says, her voice breaking.

I have compassion for my kind-hearted brother.

I listen, dazed, as Ernest, Tony, Beatrice, and Carolyn have a few minutes of whispered discussion concerning our mother's condition and what needs to be done. Carolyn and her husband leave the room to check my mother out of the hospital and make arrangements to move her into their home. Mother looks up at me with soft, reassuring eyes, and smiles. Readjusting her blanket, I will myself to be strong. I know her resolve is to make it easy on us. I also plead with Mother to consider moving home with me.

"No, Rosabelle," she says, "It would be too difficult for you to care of me . . . you have your hands full with young children at home."

This much conversation tires Mother and she appears to fall asleep. My sweet, saintly mother is dying. The good doctor estimates one to two weeks.

*Mother, I wish a train would run over me. How can it be that only now, when you are dying, I can be so aware of your suffering? I wish I had held you and praised you, told you I loved you. I want you to know that only now I realize how much you have given me in spite of my egregious shortcomings.*

I kiss her forehead and step away from her bed to wipe my tears. My brothers, with manly embarrassment, wipe tears from their eyes. The hospital room is heavy with grief. Only my blessed mother seems oblivious to her own pain. She neither requests attention, nor complains, nor explains. Occasionally she opens her eyes. She seeks no pity. She is too sick to offer comfort. She offers us acceptance.

*Mother, has it ever crossed your mind that life should have been kinder to you? Did you ever hold anyone responsible for some of your hardships, some of your heartaches? Why did you not cry out against your husband, your children, your own mother, your God?*

I say, "Here, sweet Mother, drink some water. That darn cough."

*Where did you get the strength to live when your babies died, when your husband failed you, when your sons went off to war, when your children's ignorance and selfishness clouded their understanding? I love you so, Mother.*

*I want the world to go away and leave me alone with my mother. I feel so disconnected. I need to look into her eyes. I need her hand to brush my cheek and without a word give me peace. I need her to plan how we will clean house and if we use our time effectively and the children behave, how we will be able to walk downtown, buy fabric and start dresses for my little girls before we have to start supper. I can't live without her. What will I do? I feel very vulnerable and displaced.*

There is a decision to be made—transporting Mother back to Albuquerque in an ambulance would be costly.

"She can ride in the back of my station wagon," Carolyn says.

Somewhere in childhood, in a test of wills, Carolyn's decisions were never countered. Now, here at the hospital, the rest of us do not voice our own opinion. Not one of us has the funds to pay for an ambulance. I want to speak up and say, "She is in too much pain—she needs an ambulance!" But I am quiet. On her own behalf, my mother's opinion is not sought.

Tony walks toward Mother's bed.

"I think she's asleep, Tony." I say. "Should I try to wake her?"

My brother answers, "No, no, I can't talk. I'll tell her later." He walks out of the room again.

Moments later she wakes up coughing and gasping. I call the nurse. "I don't want you to be in pain, Mother."

The nurse comes in and increases her pain medicine.

Without comment, Mother sighs deeply and dozes off again.

Though my heart is breaking, I smile brightly and in a cheerful voice say, "Two o'clock, Mom. We want to get you dressed so we can go back to Albuquerque."

While I slip the hospital gown off her shoulder, she moans. "I know it hurts to move," I say. "I'm sorry I'm so rough. I will move slower."

I support her and lean her back against the pillows, "Rest while I put your shoes on. Are you warm? Are you comfortable? It will be good to be home."

"Good," she whispers.

The orderly arrives. With little effort, he lifts my mother up and carefully positions her in a wheelchair. We wrap a blanket around her lap and legs. As we walk down the corridor of the modest hospital, staff and patients stand in the hallway and compassionately acknowledge her departure. Mother smiles. Weakly, she attempts to wave goodbye. Her demeanor projects good wishes and kindness to the people she passes. Her thoughts are with them, not with herself. My siblings and I follow behind as the orderly pushes Mother's wheelchair to the waiting car.

Denying Mother's distressed medical condition, the need for an ambulance has been rejected. Mother is made as comfortable as possible using pillows and blankets to prop her up in the back of Carolyn's car. Bea, Tony, and I follow the station wagon. Bea is driving, Tony is looking out the window, the engine is humming—and I cannot stop crying. I know if Mother saw me, she would scold me and tell me to be strong. I know if Mother saw me, I would be able to stop crying.

Finally arriving at Carolyn's house, Ernest tenderly picks Mother up from the station wagon and carries her across the lawn and up the steps to the front door. In the living room he carefully places her on the rented hospital bed. Daily, Mother slips farther and farther away. We spend our time reading to her and coaxing her to eat. We all function in a state of shock and sadness. Mother is too sick to be aware of us—too sick to be aware of our misery. My long-time friend from Taos, Lisha, is a nurse. She is here helping us with Mother's medical needs—changing the IV bottle hanging beside her bed and monitoring her pain—keeping her as comfortable as possible. Periodically, friends and relatives stop by, expressing their sorrow.

Mother acknowledges them with a weak smile. She speaks only a few words.

*I have an oppressive urgency to have my mother talk to me. I wait for her to tell me she loves me, that I'm a good person, that she understands my shortcomings—some guidance to sustain me. I wait for this illusion to pass and for the true act of living to come back. My morning, evening and night, my routine of sleep and food, my daily habits, people around me, my children—all dissolve into a void existence without a need for reason or color.*

Mother is very quiet. She is not assuring us that soon this sickness will pass and she will be up and at it, "getting somewhere." She is not imploring us with her impatience that she needs to be out of bed. She is not concerned that her work is falling behind. Her only request is that we not make her eat. She sleeps most of the time and when awake, strains to smile.

"How are you feeling, Mother?" I ask, lifting her arm to slip a clean nightgown on her. She moans, curling her arm to her chest.

"Forgive me, Mother," I say, cursing my clumsy hold on her.

Attempting to look up, she asks, "Where's Tony?"

Those are the last words I ever hear her say. Mother would never hear what Tony wanted to tell her.

Mother died three weeks after we brought her home. With little to no indication that she was leaving us, she quietly stopped breathing. My friend, Lisha, tenderly removed Mother's gold wedding band, and placed it in my hand. Crying, I clasped my fingers around the worn, golden symbol of eternity. Lisha's hand gently brushed over Mother's face, closing her eyelids. Lovingly, and with compassion, she embraced me and left the room to tell the others that Mother had passed away. I held Mother's hand. Somehow, I continued to live as her extremities grew cold. I placed my hand on her abdomen and waited with her until her body also grew cold.

The people who came to French-Fitzgerald Mortuary to pay their respects overflowed the chapel. From Taos, Santa Fe, Peñasco, Utah, Colorado, Arizona, and California they came. People I had not seen in years, some people I had forgotten and some people I had never met, all came to declare their sad goodbyes to Mother.

*Flowers! How many flowers can there be?* She would always say, "If you want to give me flowers, don't wait till I die, give them to me now that I may enjoy them."

I am distant, disconnected, and suffocating. The meaninglessness I feel is beyond understanding, beyond explaining. I want to be anywhere but here. In fact, I don't want to be anywhere. An usher insists I move from the back pew where I am sitting with my five children and husband and join my brothers and sisters at the front of the chapel near my mother's casket.

Following the service, my brothers, Ernest, Tony and Leonard, my sisters, Bea and Carolyn, and I were escorted to the lobby where we stood side-by-side, solemnly acknowledging condolences. Many share wonderful stories of how knowing our mother changed their lives and how sad they will be without her—their grief augmenting our own anguish. Hours pass before the people stop coming—an eternity!

As morning arrives, a Mass is held for Mother at Immaculate Conception Church. We follow the hearse carrying Mother. The line of cars with their lights turned on, appear to be without end. Mother is being buried in the National Veterans Military Graveyard in Santa Fe. A grave has been shoveled extra deep to accommodate my father's casket above my mother's upon *his* death. But as prayers are being read over my beloved, sainted mother's dead body, my father is intoxicated. Staggering aimlessly a short distance from the burial site, with arms flailing in all directions, his passionate and explosive feelings can be heard, full of malicious accusations, releasing his drunken, merciless, condemnations toward his dead wife's casket.

## NINE MONTHS LATER

The cold of winter has turned into summer and then to autumn so quickly. While heading to visit my dad, a whirlwind lifts and scatters the fallen leaves in front of me, and my memory slips back in time. I hear my mother singing to me as we sat on the front porch of our home in Taos so long ago:

**"Come, little leaves," said the wind one day,**
**"Come over the meadows with me, and play;**
**Put on your dresses of red and gold;**
**Summer is gone, and the days grow cold."***

---

* American poet George Cooper (1838–1927), music by Thomas J. Crawford

It's as if I can see life through my mother's eyes. I am at peace. I know that through me, my mother lives. In all that I do my mother is with me.

"Good morning, Dad," I say, as I open the door and smell the wonderful aroma of beans cooking on the stove. Mother's sewing machine is still in the same place in the living room. In my mind, I hear her voice and the humming of her machine and see her nimble fingers guiding the fabric. A deep, sad longing stirs me, remembering her sitting in the rocking chair, holding one of her grandchildren, softly lulling the baby to sleep.

I kiss my dad's forehead. My shy, gray-haired father is sitting in his recliner. Happy to see me, he tells me to serve myself some beans as he pulls out his leather pouch and, with weathered hands, firmly presses the tobacco into the bowl of his pipe.

# THE END

# EPILOGUE

T ime passes. I try to hold it, but in a blink the day is gone. And in two, a life is gone. No longer the passion for desires to be fulfilled or needs to be satisfied. It was over fifty years ago when my mother passed away and yet she is still so alive in my thoughts. She left with me, in me, a lifetime of memories that have inspired and lightened my every day.

After Mother passed away, Dad sold the parcel of land in Taos that Grandpa M.C. Martinez had given my mother. My father remained sober for the next sixteen years, content to cook his beans and attend Mass every day. While crossing the street walking home from church one day he was hit by a car. With his hip broken, he lived the rest of his life in a wheelchair. Happily receiving occasional guests, attending holiday meals with family, and nightly praying the Rosary. He quietly passed away in his home at the age of eighty-nine. He died a sober man.

Grandmother Gertrudes, at the age of eighty-six, was outside chopping pieces of firewood with a small hatchet. While walking back to the house carrying an armful of wood, she slipped on the icy steps leading up to her porch and fell, breaking her hip. She never recovered from the fall and peacefully passed away at the Holy Cross Hospital, leaving her family to mourn the life of an unparalleled, powerful matriarch.

Bea, my independent and industrious sister, married and had three wonderful children. After suffering for many years, she died before her time from a debilitating illness, leaving her oldest son to care for his two younger siblings. The beautiful Indian dolls she made of her own creation have long outlived her.

Carolyn lived a quiet life with her husband and developed a keen appreciation of art and antique furniture. She died at the age of ninety-two at a nursing home in Taos, with her son and his wife taking tender care of her.

My brother Ernest and his wife had five wonderful children. Lung cancer took my generous, kind-hearted brother at the age of eighty-two. He passed away in his Albuquerque home with two of his loving daughters at his bedside.

Tony married four times and had three children. He never pursued his exceptional artistic talent. Instead, he worked most of his life as a truck driver bringing Idaho potatoes to Albuquerque for Hutchinson Fruit Company. He died at the Holy Cross Hospital in Taos at the age of eighty-six. Both Ernest and Tony served in World War II.

My little brother, Leonard, who growing up had amenities I could only dream about, married, had three children, and died at the age of fifty-nine from complications of alcoholism. He never believed that his mother, Lenore, loved him with the same intensity that she loved all her children. Mother's grief and the story of how she gave him up to save his life were never talked about.

And as for me, I married at sixteen and had my five children by the time I turned twenty-four. Divorced after seventeen years, I stayed single for thirty-five years, vowing never to marry again. I raised my adorable family and had wonderful friends.

At the age of sixty-eight, a chance encounter brought an old friend back into my life. I had taken my sister Carolyn to lunch at a popular restaurant in Corrales when I noticed him sitting at a corner table. He told me he had lost his wife. I told him I was happy being single. We married four months later. Two people could not have needed each other more. We travelled to places around the world, entertained lavishly, and shared many special times together. Stewart left me in the Spring of 2012. With a half-drunk glass of wine sitting on his desk and a cigarette still burning in the ashtray, my sweetie stopped breathing.

Corrales is only a short drive from my home. I visit the places Stewart and I often enjoyed —the arts and crafts fair, the Fourth of July parade, and the Indigo Crow Restaurant. Sometimes I stop for lunch at the old Tijuana Bar where Dad exchanged household items for alcohol. The large man with the mustache is long gone, but his grandson now runs the place.

At the age of eighty-one, I am grateful for the privilege of health and an active lifestyle. I want to get in touch with my relatives and remember each friend I ever had. At night when I lie down, and the room is quiet, my mind is flooded with memories of my family and friends who have departed. I fall asleep talking to the spirits of my husband and my mother, assuring them that I am content and happy.

# 1913 New Mexico House of Representatives

STATE REPRESENTATIVES

1. DUNCAN McGILLIVRAY
2. JAMES V. TULLY
3. A. S. GOODELL
4. J. W. CAMPBELL
5. MIGUEL E. BACA
6. W. W. NICHOLS
7. GEORGE H. TUCKER
8. P. E. CARTER

9. J. T. EVANS
10. JOSE G. LOBATO
11. MANUEL MARTINEZ
12. W. E. ROGERS
13. REMIGIO LOPEZ
14. W. H. H. LLEWELLYN
15. MARCOS C. DE BACA
16. FLORENCE LOVE

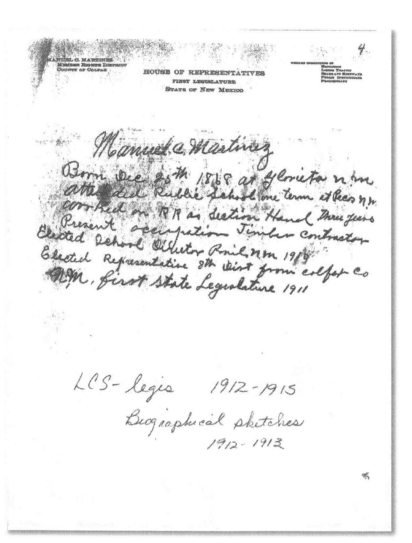

*Manuel C. Martinez*

Born Dec. 25th 1868 at Glorieta N.M. attended Public School one term at Pecos N.M. worked on RR as section Hand three years. Present occupation Timber contractor. Elected School Director Raton N.M. 1909. Elected Representative 8th Dist from Colfax Co N.M. first State Legislature 1911

LCS- legis    1912-1915
Biographical sketches
1912-1913

**Copy of Letterhead for Manuel C. Martinez,
Member Eighth District, County of Colfax**

# INDEX

# ABOUT THE AUTHOR

An active, vivacious eighty-one-year-old author, Rose Spader has seen a lifetime dream come true with the publishing of her Historical Fiction / Memoir, *Overturned Bucket*. The novel, which takes the reader on a loving, though tumultuous, journey through New Mexico history, has received an award from the New Mexico Historical Preservation Committee and was a finalist in the New Mexico/Arizona Historical contest.

With little more than an 11th grade education when she married at the age of sixteen, Rose set out to improve her family's lot. Following her mother's example, Rose knew that the only way she could break the cycle of poverty was through hard work, education, and good ethics. In addition to continuing her education and being a devoted wife and mother, Rose has worked as a waitress, a secretary, a drapery business owner, and now an author.

Today, Rose keeps a packed schedule. She is a docent for the Corrales Historical Society, speaking in the same church she attended with her mother some seventy-five years before. She stays involved with the community attending events with the Hispanic Women's Society, offering book signings, and delivering freshly baked bread to family, friends, and neighbors. In her leisure, Rose plays the piano, gardens, sews quilts, and hosts family gatherings in her Albuquerque home.

Rose is available for public speaking
and book signings at:
OverturnedBucket@gmail.com